The Complete Adventures of
Chuggalug

James McClelland

Text © James McClelland, 2013.
First published in the United Kingdom, 2013,
by Stenlake Publishing Ltd.
54–58 Mill Square, Catrine,
Ayrshire, KA5 6RD.

Printed by
Claro Print,
Unit 2.4 Kirkhill House,
81 Broom Road East,
Newton Mearns,
Glasgow,
G77 5LL

Telephone: 01290 551122
www.stenlake.co.uk

ISBN 9781840336337

The publishers regret that they cannot supply copies of any pictures featured in this book.

Since the release of his first book, *The Adventures of Chuggalug*, Jim McClelland has delighted children with his book readings, resulting in sell-out signing sessions at bookshops throughout the country.

The second book, *The Further Adventures of Chuggalug*, was equally popular with children. *The Complete Adventures of Chuggalug* is a compilation of the first two books together with many more new stories of the adventures of Chuggalug and his friends. The illustrations in this new edition are by Margaret Irving Miller.

Jim started his working life as a miner in Ayrshire and later joined the police, serving until 1995 when he began writing. He still lives in Ayrshire with his wife, Alison. The Chuggalug stories were originally bedtime stories for Jim's children and later his grandchildren.

To my wife Alison
for her patience, support and encouragement.

Contents

Chuggalug Makes a Friend 7

The Loch 23

Chuggalug and Pteranodon 42

Chuggalug Meets
Tyrannosaurus Rex 60

A Scary Adventure 73

The Return of Spring 88

Diplodocus 105

Forest Fire 127

Cousins 147

Four New Friends 168

Danger in the Caves 185

Elgin 201

Back Home 215

The Gift 230

Birthday 249

The Move 274

Chuggalug Makes a Friend

Once upon a time, in the days when dinosaurs roamed the earth, a little boy called Chuggalug lived with his mum and dad in a lovely big tree house. Chuggalug's dad had built the tree house high in the branches of a magnificent oak tree, in a clearing deep in the deepest part of the great Caledonian Forest, in a place we now call Abernethy, in a land we now know as Scotland.

Chuggalug loved the tree house. It was built of logs and had a veranda right round the outside. From his bedroom window Chuggalug could look out across the tops of the forest trees and watch the birds soaring above the forest looking for food.

At the edge of the clearing, the waters of the River Nethy sparkled in the sunshine, and gurgled over the rocks on their way to the great loch far away. In the distance he could see the dark shape of the massive mountains of Cairngorm.

One day he saw a huge flying dinosaur called a pteranadon flying low over the trees. Chuggalug leaned out of his window, fascinated by the enormous wings and the enormous beak of the pteranadon.

The pteranadon spotted Chuggalug at the window. "Aha," he squawked. "That looks like a very tasty little boy; I think I'll have him for tea."

The pteranadon swooped down, straight towards Chuggalug, who stared and stared as the huge beast came closer and closer. "Ha ha ha, hee hee hee, tonight I'll have a little boy for tea," he screeched.

Closer and closer came the monster with his great beak wide open. He was just about to snatch Chuggalug from the window when the chair he was standing on suddenly fell backwards and Chuggalug fell into his bedroom, bounced on his bed, and landed right under the table in the corner.

The pteranadon soared up into the sky, furious at missing the little boy, and went off in search of some other titbit for his tea.

Chuggalug got up from the floor and went through to the kitchen where his mum was baking some cakes.

Now Chuggalug was a good boy, and listened when his mum and dad told him that the forest was dangerous, and that he was not to wander off from the tree house alone. Sometimes, however, when he was playing a very good game, or having an exciting adventure, he would forget to be good and wander off alone.

One day Chuggalug was playing at being a hunter and was searching around the clearing for a good stick to make into a spear.

He searched further and further from the tree house, and deeper and deeper into the forest. He was so busy looking up at the trees and bushes for a good stick that he suddenly found himself falling through space.

With a crash he landed at the bottom of a deep hole in a bed of leaves. The hole was dark and damp, and had steep slippery sides, so try and try as he might, Chuggalug couldn't climb out.

He became frightened and wished that he had remembered his mum and dad's warnings about not wandering into the forest alone.

He sat down on the leaves to think about what he could do.

Then Chuggalug heard a noise. A deep groany growly sound came from the other end of the hole. He peered into the darkness. The biggest, yellowest pair of eyes he had ever seen were staring at him from the other side of the dark hole.

Chuggalug was very frightened now. He screwed up his eyes to see better and there, in the hole with him, was a huge sabre-toothed tiger.

The tiger and the boy stared at each other for ages. Why doesn't it eat me? Thought Chuggalug.

He saw the two great sabre teeth hanging from the mouth of the great beast and knew that it could eat him any time it wanted.

Once again the tiger made a soft groany growly noise. Chuggalug was still staring at the big yellow eyes when he noticed a great big tear falling from the corner of one of them.

Chuggalug looked closely at the tiger, not so frightened now, and saw that the beast was holding up one of its big furry paws. Underneath the paw, in the soft part behind the row of enormous razor-sharp claws, Chuggalug saw a large thorn sticking out.

Chuggalug could see that the sabre-toothed tiger was in pain and needed help. He crept forward towards the huge injured beast, whose head was as big as Chuggalug. He then slowly reached out and very gently pulled out the thorn from the tiger's paw.

The sabre-toothed tiger gave a

soft, deep purr of pleasure. It then stood up and came towards Chuggalug, who started to get frightened again as it came closer and closer.

It was right next to him. Chuggalug closed his eyes and thought, "This is it. This is when I get eaten."

Then he felt a huge, warm, wet, soft thing slide up his face. It was the tiger's huge, warm, wet, soft tongue licking his face. Chuggalug giggled, for the tongue was tickly. He then put his arms round the tiger's neck and gave it a great big hug.

When the tiger stood up, it was huge! Chuggalug could see that its shoulder was as high as the top of the hole. The sabre-toothed tiger lay down again and Chuggalug climbed on its broad furry back.

When the tiger stood up, Chuggalug easily climbed out of the hole onto the grass.

With one bound the sabre-toothed tiger jumped out of the hole and stood beside Chuggalug. Chuggalug looked round and realised two things all at once. It was getting dark, and he didn't know how to get home.

The big, furry sabre-toothed tiger looked down at Chuggalug, and seemed to understand.

The tiger lay down again and Chuggalug climbed on his back. The sabre-toothed tiger set off through the forest, travelling along in great leaps and bounds. Chuggalug rode along, clinging to the thick fur on its back, laughing and shouting "Boing boing, boing boing" in time with the tiger's steps.

"I know," said Chuggalug "you can be my friend. I'll call you Boing Boing."

Chuggalug's mum and dad were getting worried, and were just about to set out to look for him, when they heard the thump thump thump of a large animal running towards the tree house.

Chuggalug's dad raised his spear, ready to fight whatever it was that was running towards them. His eyes opened wide with amazement,

when he saw an enormous, fierce looking sabre-toothed tiger bounding from the forest, with Chuggalug sitting on its back, laughing and shouting.

"Dad, Dad," shouted Chuggalug, hardly taking time to draw breath, "this is my new friend. He's called Boing Boing. I pulled a thorn from his paw. He got me out of a big hole. He brought me home. Can I keep him for my pet? Can I? Can I? Please please can I?"

"Just a moment, just a moment" laughed Chuggalug's dad. "Sabre-toothed tigers are not pets. They are very fierce and dangerous wild animals, so I don't think that Boing Boing can ever be your pet."

Chuggalug started to feel very sad, but then he heard his dad say, "however, there's nothing to stop him being your friend. He will be free to roam the forest as he wants, and you can still be friends."

Chuggalug walked and skipped beside Boing Boing as the big tiger padded back towards the forest trees.

Chuggalug was a very happy and tired little boy when he went to bed that night, high up in his room in the tree house. Just before he drifted off to sleep, he heard a loud roar from the forest. But he wasn't frightened. He knew it was a friendly roar. He knew it was Boing Boing, the best friend a boy ever had.

And he just knew that they

would have many, many adventures together.

The Loch

Chuggalug was bored. It was the rainy season in the forest and he had been stuck indoors for ages and ages, while outside the rain seemed to have been pouring down for ever and ever.

He was sitting at the window of his bedroom in the tree house, gazing out across the forest, dreaming of the wonderful adventures he could have with his friend Boing Boing the sabre-toothed tiger. If only the rain would stop!

Then, suddenly, Chuggalug saw a shaft of sunlight beam down through the clouds and the rain stopped. The leaves on the trees and the grass in the clearing round the great oak tree which held the tree house were glistening in the bright sunshine.

He looked up and saw the patch of blue sky spreading and spreading, until the huge yellow sun was shining all over the forest.

Chuggalug heard the forest coming to life again. The birds started chirping and whistling. Small animals were snuffling and grunting among the trees and it seemed that the whole world was happy that the rain had stopped.

Then Chuggalug heard a loud roar from the forest.

"It's Boing Boing!" he shouted, and jumped down from the window. He ran through the house and out on to the veranda. He quickly scrambled down the rope ladder, which hung down to the ground, and ran excitedly across the grassy clearing and off into the forest.

Now his mum and dad had told Chuggalug often that the forest was dangerous, and that he should never go off alone. But he was so happy that the rain had stopped and that he was going to meet Boing Boing that he completely forgot, and anyway, it was such a lovely sunny day now after the rain. No, nothing bad could possibly happen today.

Chuggalug ran and ran, shouting for Boing Boing. Every time he heard another roar from the forest, he ran faster and faster.

Suddenly Chuggalug found himself falling through the air. He had been running so fast that he didn't see where the rain had washed the path away.

He fell and fell, tumbling over and over, and landed with a teeth-rattling bump. But he didn't stop. He slithered and slipped down the steep slope. He slid faster and faster down the muddy slide, rushing round corners and down and down until, with a mighty splash, he plunged into the river, fast flowing and deep, with the flood waters swirling all around him.

Chuggalug was swept along helplessly. The rushing, roaring water whirled him round and round, over and over until he didn't know which way was which.

Chuggalug was very scared. He was gasping for breath. The water was over his head. He struggled to reach the surface to get some air. Just when he thought he would never breathe again, he felt a bump and caught hold of a gnarled old tree trunk, which was being washed downriver by the raging floodwater

Slowly and painfully, Chuggalug pulled himself out of the water on to the tree trunk. He lay on his tummy among the branches, holding on tightly in case he fell back into the brown swirling water.

On and on he drifted, sometimes sleeping; sometimes

awake, wondering if he would ever see his mum and dad again.

He was lying with his eyes closed, resting his head on the tree trunk when he realised that the water was calmer, slower and quieter. "Good," he thought, opening his eyes and sitting up. "I'll be able to swim to the riverbank."

But the riverbank wasn't there anymore! Chuggalug looked all round. With horror he saw that the tree trunk was drifting out into the middle of a great loch, carrying him along with it.

The dark waters of the loch were surrounded on both sides by high, steeply sloping mountains.

Then Chuggalug remembered his dad telling him about a great loch,

whose dark waters were surrounded by steep mountains. It was called Loch Ness and was a dangerous place.

He tried to paddle the tree trunk towards the side of the loch, desperately paddling with his hands and his feet. But the tree trunk was too heavy. He drifted on slowly towards the middle of the loch. The banks of the loch were getting smaller and smaller and slowly disappeared into the mist until, everywhere Chuggalug looked, he could see nothing but water all around him.

It was very still and quiet, only the sound of the water lapping against the tree trunk disturbing the silence. Chuggalug shouted for help, but he knew that he was so far away from the side of the loch that no one could possibly hear him.

He was lying on his tummy, slowly paddling with his hands. His face was near the surface of the water. He was watching the small ripples on the water, wondering how he could get back to the shore and thinking that it must be about lunchtime and he was getting hungry.

Suddenly there was a disturbance on the surface, close to his face, and there, right in front of him was the biggest head Chuggalug had ever seen.

It was a huge scaly head with two enormous green eyes, and they were looking at him curiously and closely.

But even more frightening was the mouth. The beast's head was massive and Chuggalug knew that that huge mouth could easily swallow him up

He tried not to scream. He didn't want to startle the monster, which was still watching him closely.

It was very difficult not to scream when the head started to rise out of the water on a long scaly neck. At the same time another head appeared beside Chuggalug, just as big as the first one, and started to sniff him.

Chuggalug sat up on the tree trunk to look at the monsters. Both beasts silently disappeared beneath the water. Chuggalug stared at the ripples on the surface and wondered if he had been dreaming. To his amazement a third head rose out of the water beside him.

This one didn't frighten Chuggalug. It was much smaller than the other two and was obviously a baby monster.

"Hello," said the little monster, watching Chuggalug curiously, its head slightly tilted to one side, "what are you?"

"I'm a boy," replied Chuggalug "and I'm stuck out here on this tree trunk. What are you and who are those other two big monsters? Please ask them not to eat me."

"I'm a plesiosaur," said the small beast, "and that's my mum and dad.

We live in the loch. We won't eat you. I'll get my dad. He'll help you."

Then the two large plesiosaurs reappeared, their huge heads rising out of the water on their long necks, high above Chuggalug.

"Well then, boy," said the daddy plesiosaur, slowly and sternly, "how did you get yourself into this fix? I don't suppose your mum and dad know where you are."

"No, they don't," said Chuggalug quietly, "and if I'd done what they told me and not ran off into the forest alone, I wouldn't be here."

"Exactly!" said the mummy plesiosaur. "Little boys and little plesiosaurs" she said, casting a quick glance at her own little monster, who developed a sudden interest in the sky, "should always listen to their parents. It would keep them out of lots of trouble."

"Now then," said the daddy plesiosaur, "how can we help you? We can push you to the shore, but you'll have to get home through the forest by yourself. Do you know the way home?"

"No. I don't." Chuggalug was feeling very sorry for himself and felt very silly for not doing as his mum and dad had told him.

"Well, let's get you to the side of the loch and on to dry land first." The daddy plesiosaur swam behind the tree trunk, pushing it easily towards the shore of the loch.

They had almost reached the shore, with the mummy and baby plesiosaurs swimming alongside, when they all heard a huge, deep roar from the forest, near the side of the loch.

"Oh dear," said mummy plesiosaur looking very worried. "How will you ever get home through the forest with all the wild animals roaming about? Whatever can we do?"

"Don't worry," cried Chuggalug, laughing with relief. "I can see the wild animal. It's my friend Boing Boing the sabre-toothed tiger. I'll be all right now. He'll take me home safely."

The tree trunk bumped against the shore and Chuggalug jumped on to the land. He turned back to the three monsters. "Thank you very much for helping me." He said, watching the two big plesiosaurs slowly disappear under the water.

The little one was still watching him. "I hope you can come back to the loch one day." He called to Chuggalug, his head slowly sinking into the loch on his long neck. "I've never met a boy before. We could have some fun."

"Okay I'll try to come back," shouted Chuggalug. "I've never met a plesiosaur before. My dad says this loch is called Loch Ness. I'll call you Nessie, and we can be friends."

"Goodbye Chuggalug. See you soon."

"Goodbye Nessie." The water was still again as the small plesiosaur disappeared. Chuggalug turned towards Boing Boing, who was walking towards him.

"Come on Chuggalug," said Boing Boing, "jump on my back and let's get you home before it gets dark. I followed you down the river when you fell in, but I couldn't follow you out on to the loch."

Chuggalug climbed on to the big tiger's back. He took a last look back at the dark waters of the loch and hoped that he could come back some day to see his new friend Nessie.

Boing Boing soon had Chuggalug back in the clearing, and watched him run over to the rope ladder and climb up into the tree house.

Chuggalug ran through to his bedroom and over to the window to watch as Boing Boing padded off into the forest.

He then took a deep breath and slowly walked towards the kitchen, to explain to his mum and dad about his wet clothes, and tell them about his adventure in Loch Ness and about his new friend Nessie.

Chuggalug and Pteranadon

Chuggalug was playing with his cart. It was a wooden cart, with four wooden wheels. His dad had made it for him. Chuggalug thought it was the best cart in the world and loved pulling it along by the vine rope attached to the front.

He was lying on his back in the cart with his arms hanging over the sides, half dozing in the warm sunshine, remembering the days he spent, sitting by his dad's side, watching him build it.

He had watched him shape the wheels and fit them to the cart. He remembered that nice feeling, knowing that his dad was building it

especially for him. Chuggalug always enjoyed remembering that feeling.

As he sat there, his gaze drifted round the clearing under the giant oak tree. It was the tallest in the forest, and held the tree house in its topmost branches. His slowly wandering eyes rested on his friend Boing Boing, the huge sabre-toothed tiger, who was asleep at the edge of the clearing. Chuggalug could hear the deep purring from the tiger as it slept.

Boing Boing was not easy to spot, his stripy coat mingling with the dappled yellow sunlight falling through the gently rustling leaves of the trees on to the grass.

Lying lazily in his cart, Chuggalug had an idea. It would be fun to play a trick on Boing Boing and give him a fright. He remembered that his dad had told him never ever to startle a sleeping animal, whether it was a dog, a cat, a dinosaur or anything but, as boys and girls often do, he thought that "just this once" it would be fun.

He climbed out of the cart and, pulling it along behind him, crept quietly across the clearing to where Boing Boing was sleeping. As he got close to the tiger the deep purring was louder and louder as the huge animal slept peacefully in the warm sunshine.

Chuggalug smiled to himself as he thought of the trick he was going to play. Although he didn't really think he was being naughty or bad he glanced back towards the tree house to make sure his mum and dad weren't watching.

He tiptoed up to Boing Boing and, as quietly as he could, tied the vine rope to the big tiger's tail. He then crept back to the cart and climbed in. Trying not to laugh, Chuggalug picked up a stick from the ground and, with a loud yell, which shattered the silence in the clearing, threw the stick at Boing Boing, hitting him on the back of the head.

As all boys and girls know, there is a time when you are being naughty when you suddenly wish you hadn't, and this was that time for Chuggalug.

When the stick hit him on the head, Boing Boing leapt to his feet and, hearing the loud noise behind him, ran off into the forest without looking round, away from whatever danger was behind him. He was confused and realised that something had a grip of his tail and was running after him, and it was running just as fast as he was.

Boing Boing ran faster and faster, and farther and farther into the forest. He was running blindly, trying to outrun the thing behind him and had no idea where he was running to.

Chuggalug had fallen backwards into the cart when Boing Boing started to run and was now being tossed about, this way and that, upside down and round about. He was yelling for Boing Boing to stop but the noise of the cart's wooden wheels rattling and crashing on the stones and branches was so loud that the huge tiger couldn't hear him.

Boing Boing was roaring like thunder and all the little animals were scuttling and scattering out of the way as the great beast crashed through the forest, the wooden cart, with Chuggalug in it, clattering along behind.

Then it happened! Suddenly the forest cleared and Boing Boing found himself running towards the edge of a huge cliff. He turned quickly and ran back towards the trees.

The cart hit a large boulder at the cliff edge and smashed into a thousand pieces. Chuggalug was thrown high into the air and straight over the edge of the cliff.

He found himself falling, tumbling over and over, towards the jagged rocks far, far below. He was screaming and shouting but he knew that no one could hear him, or help him.

The rocks came rushing up to meet him and Chuggalug closed his eyes. He felt the wind blowing against his face and through his hair as he fell faster and faster.

Then something very strange happened. Chuggalug felt himself stop falling. He seemed to be flying up into the air. He opened his eyes and saw the rocks far below him. He was soaring high above them, getting higher and higher. He could see the cliff and the forest trees getting smaller and smaller below him and started to laugh with relief.

He stopped laughing when he saw why he hadn't crashed into the rocks, and why he was flying high into the sky. An enormous pteranadon had him in its beak and was carrying him high above the forest. He looked round to see where it was taking him and his heart sank. Ahead he could see the pteranadon's massive nest, high up on a ledge, near the top of a mountain.

"Oh dear!" thought Chuggalug. "I'm for it now. The pteranadon is taking me to its nest to eat me. If only Boing Boing was here to save me." He was very scared and really wished he hadn't played such a cruel trick on his best friend.

The pteranadon flew on towards its nest, carrying poor Chuggalug in its beak. As it landed on the ledge near the top of the mountain, it dropped Chuggalug, with a bump, into the bottom of the huge nest.

Chuggalug had his eyes closed again as he tumbled into the nest. He heard lots of squawking and squealing and opened his eyes. He was sitting in the bottom of the nest surrounded by four baby pteranodons.

"Mum! Mum! What is that thing?" squawked one of the babies, poking curiously at Chuggalug with its beak.

"Hey! That tickles," shouted Chuggalug, falling backwards into the bottom of the nest, giggling.

The baby pteranodons, seeing Chuggalug laughing, all started to cackle and laugh too.

"It's a baby human, and I think he's in trouble." The mummy pteranadon was trying to keep her voice stern amidst all the giggling and laughing. "If I hadn't spotted him falling over the cliff and caught him, I don't know what would have happened."

The baby pteranodons stopped laughing and looked at Chuggalug curiously.

"Can't you fly?" asked one.

"Where are your wings?" said the second.

"How do you eat with no beak?" squawked the third.

"How did you fall over a cliff?" asked the fourth.

Chuggalug took a deep breath and told them the whole story, from tying the rope to Boing Boing's tail, to landing in their nest. At the end of the story he was feeling very sorry for himself and was struggling not to cry.

"Well!" said the mummy pteranadon. "I hope your friend the tiger is all right after the fright you gave him. I don't suppose he expected his best friend to do such a thing. Do you?" she said, looking sternly at Chuggalug.

"N n no." He stammered. "I don't think he would. Do you think he'll still be my friend?"

"I really wouldn't know," replied the mummy pteranadon "but I think I'd better try to get you home before it gets dark."

Chuggalug couldn't tell the mummy pteranadon how to get back to the tree house in the forest where he lived. He had bounced about in the cart behind Boing Boing for so long that he had no idea which direction they had come or how far they had travelled.

The mummy pteranadon gave him a rather worried look. "I'll just have to take you back to the cliff where I found you. Perhaps you'll

remember from there."

Chuggalug said goodbye to the baby pteranodons, who said they would try to find his tree house and visit him once they learned how to fly. The mummy pteranadon then picked him up in her enormous beak and soared over the forest, back towards the cliff.

Chuggalug scanned the treetops below, looking for familiar signs which might guide him home. But everything was strange and he began to think he would never get home again.

Then, as they flew down towards the top of the cliff, Chuggalug heard a loud roar from below.

"Listen!" he shouted. "That's Boing Boing!" He looked down and there at the edge of the forest, near the cliff he saw the huge sabre-toothed tiger looking up at them.

"Okay. I'll fly low over him and drop you beside him, and I hope you'll tell him how sorry you are for the way you treated him."

"I will, and thank you for saving me" shouted Chuggalug as the great flying dinosaur swooped low over the ground, gently dropping him on the grass next to Boing Boing, and soared away, high into the blue sky.

As she disappeared, Chuggalug slowly turned and looked at Boing Boing who was standing quietly looking down at him. He ran to the great beast, threw his arms round his neck and buried his face into the warm thick fur of his chest.

"I'm sorry Boing Boing. I've been really horrible. Will you still be my friend, please? I'll never do anything like that again."

He looked up at Boing Boing, who was still quiet. Then the big tiger bent down towards Chuggalug and licked his face with his enormous soft wet tongue. Chuggalug was so happy he just laughed and laughed, and hugged Boing Boing as tightly as he could.

"Right. Let's get you home, laddie" said Boing Boing, crouching down so that Chuggalug could climb on to his back. They padded off through the forest, back to the clearing with the great oak tree, which held the tree house where Chuggalug lived with his mum and dad.

Chuggalug climbed down from the tiger's back and, waving goodbye to his friend, ran over to the rope ladder and climbed up into the tree house.

"Is that you Chuggalug?" he heard his mum call from the kitchen. "Wash your hands and come through for supper."

He washed his hands slowly and thoughtfully. He wasn't looking forward to telling his mum and dad about the cart, the cliff and the pteranadons.

Chuggalug Meets Tyrannosaurus Rex

Chuggalug was looking for Boing Boing. They were playing at hide-and-seek. Boing Boing was very difficult to find in the forest. He was a huge sabre-toothed tiger and was Chuggalug's best friend. His yellow and black stripes made him very hard to see when he lay hiding in the bushes in the dappled sunshine.

Chuggalug crept through the forest as quietly as he could, listening for the slightest sound to give him a clue to where Boing Boing was hiding. He would creep forward for a time, then stop and stand perfectly still and listen for ages. He heard nothing but

the normal forest noises: the soft wind rustling the leaves on the trees, and the whistles and screeches of small animals far off through the forest – but no Boing Boing.

"Boing Boing is too good at this game," thought Chuggalug as he stood listening in a clearing. "I wish I could find him, then it will be my turn to hide, and I'll make sure he doesn't find me for ages."

Then he heard it!

He cocked his ear up and listened very carefully.

Yes, there it was again, a soft purring sound. It was coming from a clump of bushes just in front of him, so Chuggalug sneaked forward, parted the bushes and peered in.

There, in the centre of the clump, lay Boing Boing, his huge head resting on his front paws, fast asleep.

With a shout, Chuggalug lunged into the bushes and dived on Boing Boing's back, threw his arms round the great furry neck and yelled, "I've found you, I've found you. Now it's my turn to go and hide."

Boing Boing got up and, with a loud roar, stretched himself, the way sabre-toothed tigers do. He then sat up and closed his eyes so that Chuggalug could run off and hide.

Chuggalug ran and ran as fast as his legs would carry him, farther and farther into the deepest and darkest part of the forest. He was so determined that Boing Boing would not find him that he had no idea how far he was running, or where he was running to.

Eventually Chuggalug found a thick clump of bushes, at the edge of a clearing in the forest that looked perfect to hide in. He looked round about and realised that he was in a strange part of the forest, a part of the forest that his dad had often told him to stay away from. He frowned, feeling slightly uneasy for a moment. But then he thought, "it'll be alright, just this once, and anyway, Boing Boing will find me soon and it'll be okay."

He pushed his way into the bushes and sat down quietly to wait for Boing Boing to find him.

He listened for Boing Boing coming, but he really knew that he wouldn't hear him because the huge tiger could pad silently through the forest and Chuggalug never ever heard him coming.

Then Chuggalug heard a deep booming sound away in the distance. Boom, boom, boom, boom, far away, but getting closer. "What can that be?" he wondered aloud.

Boom, boom, boom, boom, closer still. "I know," he thought nervously, "it's Boing Boing looking for me, and he's making that noise so I won't think it's him." He smiled to himself and snuggled deeper into the bushes.

BOOM, BOOM, BOOM,

BOOM. It was really close now. Chuggalug could feel the ground shaking underneath him, and was getting a bit frightened. "I hope it is Boing Boing, I don't know what it can be if it's not."

BOOM, BOOM, BOOM, BOOM. The ground was really shaking now and Chuggalug knew that it wasn't Boing Boing.

He crawled to the edge of the bushes, slowly parted them with his hands, and looked out.

For the first time, Chuggalug was face to face with tyrannosaurus rex, one of the biggest, fiercest dinosaurs of them all.

Chuggalug watched fixed to the spot, as the gigantic beast looked round the clearing. He stood very still, as his dad had once told him that most dinosaurs had poor eyesight, and that if you didn't move, they probably wouldn't see you. He also remembered that his dad had told him to stay out of this part of the forest, and wished that he had done as he was told.

It seemed that his dad was right, as the huge dinosaur didn't seem to see him and was still standing up, it's head as high as the top branches of the trees, looking round the clearing.

Chuggalug was just starting to feel slightly better, and to think that maybe the tyrannosaurus wouldn't find him after all, when he felt himself start to lose his balance. He had leaned too far forward. He desperately tried to get his balance, but suddenly tumbled out, with a crash, into the clearing, right in front of tyrannosaurus rex.

The dinosaur turned round quickly, and let out a giant roar. It bent down and looked at Chuggalug as he lay on the grass at the feet of the monster. It let out another roar, and Chuggalug could smell its hot horrible breath and see its rows of huge teeth as its great mouth opened above him.

Chuggalug closed his eyes, gulped and tried to shout for help, but he seemed to have lost his voice and couldn't make a sound.

Just as he was sure he was going

to be eaten, he heard another great roar from the side of the clearing.

This was a different roar, one that Chuggalug knew. He opened his eyes and saw Boing Boing leap, with one mighty bound, high over him and sink his teeth into the giant dinosaur's nose.

"I suppose you think that's funny," squealed the dinosaur, rubbing its nose with its front feet.

"Yes I do," laughed Chuggalug, finding his voice again and jumping to his feet. Boing Boing ran round and bit the dinosaur's tail. The huge dinosaur let out another roar and thundered off into the forest, wondering how it could lick its nose and tail at the same time.

Chuggalug laughed and climbed onto Boing Boing's back.

"Let's get you home," said the big tiger and bounded off through the forest, back to the clearing where Chuggalug lived with his mum and dad in a tree house his dad had built, high in the branches of a huge oak tree.

Chuggalug jumped down from Boing Boing's back, gave the tiger a big hug, and said, "You're the best friend a boy could ever have."

He ran over to the rope ladder, which took him up into the tree house. "Is that you Chuggalug?" his mum called as she heard him come in. "Where have you been? Your supper is nearly ready."

"Oh, I was just outside playing with Boing Boing," called Chuggalug as he washed his hands. After all his mum would only worry if he told her about his adventure with Boing Boing and T-Rex.

A Scary Adventure

Chuggalug was very good at climbing trees. He had plenty of trees to practise on, living, as he did, in the great forest that, even from the topmost branches of the tallest trees, stretched in every direction as far as the eye could see.

He had a favourite tree to climb. It was a great oak tree whose branches spread out wider than all the other trees around it. The topmost branch was very strong, and had two small branches just at the right height for Chuggalug to stand on, holding on with one hand, to scan the treetops all round.

The branch would sway gently

in the breeze, but Chuggalug wasn't scared as he knew it was strong enough to hold him. He loved making the branch swing by leaning one way, then the other, but he always held on tight with one hand.

Chuggalug often wondered what his mum would say if she saw him swinging high above the ground in the high branches of the great oak tree. He would laugh to himself because he knew that it was his secret tree in his secret part of the forest.

One day Chuggalug was out in the forest looking for his best friend Boing Boing, the huge and ferocious looking sabre-toothed tiger who also lived in the forest.

Chuggalug and Boing Boing

had been best friends ever since the day when Chuggalug had found the huge tiger in pain with a large thorn in his foot, and had pulled it out. They had had many adventures together since then and Boing Boing had become Chuggalug's guardian in the forest, keeping him out of trouble when he could, and rescuing him when he couldn't.

After looking and looking for ages and ages, Chuggalug had a good idea. He would go to his favourite oak tree and climb to the top. He could then call to Boing Boing from up there and he would hear him and come running. He ran through the forest, kicking up the piles of golden leaves that lay like a thick carpet on the ground, until at last he reached the great oak tree.

The bottom branches of the tree looked much too high for Chuggalug to reach, but he found a stick lying on the ground and, catching the twigs at the end of the bottom branch, pulled the end down until he could jump up and grab the leaves and pull the branch down. He worked his way along the branch towards the trunk of the tree and, when the branch was thick enough to hold him, he caught hold of it with both hands swinging his legs up and over the branch. He pulled himself up and sat on the branch.

Now came the part Chuggalug loved. The branches of the oak tree were all just the right thickness for his foot to stand on or his hand to hold on to, and in no time at all he had reached the top of the tree.

He shaded his eyes from the bright autumn sun with his free hand and looked all around. He felt as if he was at the top of the world, for he could see the forest treetops like a green and gold carpet covering the world below him. The bright blue sky above, dusted with cotton wool clouds, became the ceiling. Chuggalug felt as if he was the only person in the whole world.

He then started to swing the branch back and forwards, faster and faster, yelling, "Boing Boing, Boing Boing," in time to the swing of the branch. After a few moments Chuggalug heard a loud roar away in the distance and yelled louder still, "Boing Boing, Boing Boing."

The roar came again, this time louder and closer, but this time Chuggalug stopped shouting and kept very quiet. That wasn't Boing Boing. It sounded much bigger and not very friendly.

Another huge roar, this time very close, and Chuggalug could feel the oak tree shaking. He looked down and there, at the bottom of the tree was a dinosaur with a huge head and the biggest mouth of any dinosaur he had ever seen. It was allosaurus, just as fierce, but much much bigger than tyrannosaurus rex.

The enormous beast had heard Chuggalug yelling and was standing up on its hind legs, looking up into the branches of the tree, snorting and grunting now and then as if it was talking to itself or wondering where the noise had come from.

Chuggalug kept perfectly still, for his dad had told him that dinosaurs had poor eyesight, and could only see you if you moved. It seemed to be working. Allosaurus slowly walked round the tree, but obviously could not see or hear Chuggalug, who was being very quiet and very still.

Then he felt the sneeze coming! As he put his free hand up to his nose, the dinosaur saw the movement and looked up quickly.

It all happened at the same time. The dinosaur let out an enormous roar that shook the oak tree. Chuggalug could see the huge open mouth below him as he sneezed and lost his grip on the branch. He fell straight down into the monstrous mouth of the dinosaur, narrowly missing the razor sharp teeth. He slid down and down the long slippery tunnel of its throat falling with a bump into the great dark cavern of its tummy.

Chuggalug looked around him. It was completely dark and he could see nothing. He was very frightened and couldn't imagine how he was going to get out.

The dinosaur let out a great roar and, as its mouth opened, a ray of light showed him the way back up the tunnel he had just slid down.

Chuggalug picked up a piece of bone that was lying beside him and began to crawl to the bottom of the dark tunnel that was the dinosaur's throat.

Allosaurus continued to roar and roar, which was good because it let Chuggalug see where he was going. It also let him see the rows of huge teeth in the dinosaur's mouth. He had no idea how he was going to get past them and get out.

All of a sudden Chuggalug was thrown from side to side, as the monster seemed to swing round, first one way then the other. The roaring got louder and louder.

Chuggalug crawled slowly up towards the dinosaur's enormous mouth. It was roaring all the time now, and was swinging violently from side to side. He realised that the huge beast was in a fight.

He was nearly at the mouth of the dinosaur when he had a horrible thought. What if I get out and find that it's fighting an even bigger dinosaur?

He was at the back of the dinosaur's mouth now and could see its great big tonsils dangling at the back of its throat. He swung the piece of bone and stuck it into the side of the dinosaur's throat.

It was only a tiny piece of bone compared to the size of the dinosaur and Chuggalug thought the beast wouldn't feel it but, suddenly, he felt the huge beast draw in its breath. It let out a gigantic cough, and Chuggalug felt himself being carried forward, tumbling over and over, and finally being blown out of the dinosaur's mouth, landing with a thump on the ground.

Allosaurus was very angry now, and Chuggalug looked round to see what it had been fighting. There, behind the back of the great monster was Boing Boing.

As allosaurus peered down at the ground where Chuggalug lay, Boing Boing called out, "Get ready,

Chuggalug," and sank his teeth into the dinosaur's thrashing tail.

The dinosaur twisted round and Boing Boing bounded over to Chuggalug, who jumped up and onto the tiger's back. He held on tightly as Boing Boing raced off through the forest, leaving the roaring dinosaur far behind.

Boing Boing ran and ran, and Chuggalug laughed and laughed with relief until they reached the edge of the clearing and the tree house, which was Chuggalug's home.

Chuggalug climbed down from Boing Boing's back and, giving him a big hug, waved goodbye to the big tiger as he ran across the clearing to the oak tree. He climbed up the rope ladder into the tree house and ran to his bedroom.

He ran to the window and watched Boing Boing disappearing into the forest far below and thought about the narrow escape he'd just had. He realised that this oak tree with his tree house in it was really his favourite tree after all.

The Return of Spring

Chuggalug was looking forward to the time when the snow and rain stopped. That was the time when he would see his best friend, Boing Boing again.

Every year when the forest became dark and the snow came, Chuggalug's dad would pull up the rope ladder to the tree house, built high in the branches of the great oak tree in the middle of the clearing in the forest. Chuggalug and his mum and dad would stay up there, safe above the deep snowdrifts and the floods when the snow turned to rain.

At the same time Boing Boing would disappear. Boing Boing was a large sabre-toothed tiger who was

Chuggalug's best friend.

Chuggalug knew that Boing Boing disappeared when the snows came and that the great tiger went far away to a place where it did not get so cold as it did in this part of the forest.

He also knew that, in the spring, when the forest came back to life, Boing Boing would return and they would again have many adventures together as before.

At long last the forest was now coming back to life. Chuggalug sat on his bed in the tree house, looking out of the window and across the treetops to the great dark mountains far away. The sun was shining and the air was filled with the fresh smells of the new forest: the new leaves, the new flowers, the sounds of the forest animals awakening and the chirping, grunting, and snorting as they searched for food or busied themselves building a den or a nest.

Chuggalug saw something moving below in the clearing. He looked down and saw to his delight, far below, his dad was standing in the clearing waving to him. Chuggalug whooped with joy, ran out of his bedroom and jumped onto the rope ladder which stretched down all the way to the grassy clearing far below.

"Be careful!" called his mum, laughing at his eagerness to get down the ladder, "and don't go off into the forest until your dad has made sure it's safe."

"Okay, mum, I won't," Chuggalug called back as he scampered down the rope ladder. He jumped off before he reached the bottom and landed with a thump and a laugh on the soft grass below.

"Steady," laughed his dad as he saw Chuggalug land on the grass and run off as fast as he could round the clearing. "Stay in the clearing until I have a chance to take a look around."

"Okay," shouted Chuggalug, just before he tripped, fell and rolled over and over, landing on his back, laughing up at the blue sky and the wonderful bright sunshine.

After a while, his dad came back into the clearing. "It's alright," he called to Chuggalug. "There are no dinosaurs to be seen, but don't wander off into the forest."

"Can I go and look for Boing Boing?" pleaded Chuggalug, who was so looking forward to seeing his friend again. "Can I please, dad?"

"No," said his dad. "Boing Boing will come to see you when he's ready. We have no idea where he'll be at the moment, so just stay in the clearing and play."

So Chuggalug played in the clearing. He lay down on the grass and rolled down the grassy bank, to the edge of the river, which sparkled and gurgled over the stones. He threw stones into the river, and tried to make the flat stones skim over the surface. He played and played all day, stopping every now and then to look round the forest at the edge of the clearing, and listen for any signs of Boing Boing. But Boing Boing still hadn't appeared when he heard his mum call to him that it was time to come in for bed.

"Oh well," said his dad, seeing Chuggalug's sad face and patting him on the head. "I expect Boing Boing will be here tomorrow or the next day. But you must remember that he is a wild animal, and you'll just have to be patient until he comes back."

"I suppose so," said Chuggalug in a tired voice. "I just hope he comes back soon."

But day after day went slowly by, and Boing Boing did not come back.

Chuggalug was very sad. Days had turned into weeks and his friend still hadn't returned. Chuggalug wandered around in the forest, kicking the leaves on the ground, wondering why Boing Boing hadn't come.

"Maybe I wasn't a good enough friend," he thought sadly, and Boing Boing has found a new best friend. As more and more days passed he got sadder and sadder and sadder.

One night after Chuggalug had spent ages sitting at his bedroom window looking out over the forest, hoping Boing Boing would appear, his dad came in and sat down beside him. He explained to Chuggalug that sometimes wild animals got into fights with other animals and could be injured or even killed and that it could be that something had happened to Boing Boing which kept him from coming to see Chuggalug.

"I'm never going to see him again," said Chuggalug, feeling the tears rise to his eyes. He buried his face in his pillow and eventually fell fast asleep.

When Chuggalug woke up it was still nighttime. The house was quiet and he could see the big yellow moon and the stars out of the window. He was wondering what had wakened him when he heard it. Far in the distance a great roar echoed through the forest.

Chuggalug knew that roar. It

was Boing Boing.

He jumped out of bed and ran to the rope ladder. He rushed down the ladder and ran off into the forest. He could see by the light of the moon, and just beyond the edge of the clearing there was Boing Boing walking towards him.

Chuggalug ran forward and threw his arms round the great tiger's neck. He hugged him and hugged him, and he could hear the deep purring noise as he buried his face into the warm fur in Boing Boing's chest.

"Where have you been?" asked Chuggalug. "I thought something had happened to you and I would never see you again."

"Come with me and I'll show you," said Boing Boing, laughing.

The huge tiger bent down so that Chuggalug could climb on to his back. Boing Boing then bounded off through the trees, into the thickest part of the forest.

They ran and ran until daylight began to break and Chuggalug could see that they were near the bottom of the great mountains that he had often seen from his bedroom window.

Chuggalug knew that he had never been as far away from the tree house before. He was still wondering where Boing Boing was taking him when the big sabre-toothed tiger stopped.

Chuggalug climbed down and

looked around. "What is it?" he asked, curiously. "Why have you brought me all this way?"

Boing Boing gently nudged Chuggalug with his big wet nose, pushing him forward until Chuggalug saw that there was a cave opening in front of him, right at the bottom of the mountain.

Boing Boing nudged him right to the mouth of the cave, and Chuggalug peered in. It was very dark in the cave and, at first he could see nothing. Then, as his eyes became accustomed to the dark, Chuggalug saw something move.

He was looking at another huge sabre-toothed tiger, and was just about to turn and run when he was knocked on to his back by first one, then two, then three, then four squealing bundles of fur which landed on his chest.

Chuggalug saw that he had been attacked by four beautiful little sabre-toothed tiger cubs, which were now pushing and jostling each other, all trying to lick his face at the same time.

"So this is why you couldn't come earlier," he laughed to Boing Boing as the small wet tongues tickled his face. "You had to look after your cubs."

Chuggalug stood up and saw that the female sabre-toothed tiger had come to the mouth of the cave and was lying with her huge furry head resting on her front paws,

watching him playing with the cubs.

It was a very happy and tired little boy who eventually untangled himself from the squealing bundle of tiger cubs and climbed on to Boing Boing's back for the journey home.

Back in the tree house, after waving to Boing Boing as he bounded back into the forest, Chuggalug ran to tell his mum and dad about the four lovely tiger cubs.

"Well," said his dad "So that's why Boing Boing didn't come earlier. But you must remember that he might not be able to come here so often if he has cubs to look after."

But Chuggalug didn't mind. He now knew that Boing Boing was safe and well and still his friend, and that he would have many games and adventures with the cubs in the days ahead.

Diplodocus

It was a warm, sunny and peaceful day in the great Caledonian Forest, long long ago, in the days when dinosaurs roamed the Earth. Chuggalug was wandering home beside the clear cool waters of a river, stopping sometimes to throw a stick into the river, or to skim a flat stone across the sparkling surface of a pool.

Sometimes he would hear the rumbles and roars of enormous dinosaurs crashing through the undergrowth far below, reminding him how dangerous the forest was, and of his mum and dad's warnings about not going too far from the tree house alone.

Chuggalug wasn't a bad boy, and usually remembered to be careful, and not to wander off alone. Today, however, he had been having such fun sailing twigs down the river that, although he had started in a pool next to the tree house clearing, he had chased his pretend boats further and further down the river, and had wandered deep into the forest, far away from the tree house.

He stood on a stone at the edge of a deep, smooth pool in the river, quietly watching two of his make believe stick boats drifting slowly downstream. He had just decided that he should probably start to make his way home when he heard it.

He stood absolutely still and

listened. He heard it again. The sharp crack as someone, or something, in the forest behind him, stood on a dry twig and snapped it.

Chuggalug slowly and quietly looked round. The forest was silent. He scanned the bushes at the side of the river. He screwed up his eyes and peered into the gloom of the forest. Then he spotted not one, but two pairs of eyes silently watching him through the leaves of the bushes behind him.

Chuggalug had no idea who, or what was watching him, but he did know that it was probably unfriendly and dangerous, and that he was far from home. He began to sneak, slowly and silently along the river's edge, back towards the tree house. He could see that, as he moved along the riverbank, the two sets of eyes were following him. When he moved, they moved. When he stopped, they stopped.

Chuggalug became frightened, and wished that he had been more careful and not wandered off from the tree house. He was even more frightened when, through a gap in the bushes, he saw what was following him. Two dinosaurs walked quietly from bush to bush watching him. They were about the same height as Chuggalug and walked upright, leaning slightly forward as they went.

The weight of their speckled brown bodies was perfectly balanced by their small muscular tails. The sight of the large black razor sharp claws on their back feet and the long hooked claws on their front feet made Chuggalug's blood run cold. They were velociraptors, the fastest, the fiercest and the most cunning of all the dinosaurs.

Chuggalug wished that his best friend Boing Boing was with him, but Boing Boing was not there. Chuggalug was alone.

He crouched down at the edge of the river to think. He knew that if he tried to run away, the velociraptors would hear him and catch him easily. He just had to get far enough away from them without them hearing him, and make a run for it. He looked around and saw that the river at this point was gurgling over the rocks and was quite shallow.

Chuggalug quietly waded out to the middle of the river and started to make his way upstream slowly and carefully, hoping that the two dinosaurs wouldn't notice him. He seemed to have sneaked up the river for ages and ages and decided that it was time to make a run for it.

He splashed out of the river, on to the bank and ran as fast as his legs would carry him, away from the velociraptors, through the forest towards the tree house and safety.

He heard the loud screeches of the velociraptors behind him. They were furious. Their high-pitched

screams and roars echoed through the trees as they gave chase. "After him! After him! He's getting away!" screeched one. "Get him! Get him! You go that way. I'll go this way" screamed the other. They split up and galloped through the thick ferns after Chuggalug.

He was running as fast as a boy could run, crashing through bushes and ferns, and leaping over fallen branches, but he knew that the velociraptors were running faster and were gaining on him step by step.

They were getting closer and closer behind him. The screeching became louder and louder, higher and higher, as the horrible creatures called to each other, and became more and more excited as they realised they were catching Chuggalug

"Ah ha, we're catching him, we're catching him" squealed one.

"Yes! Yes! We'll have him soon. I knew he wouldn't get away" squawked the other.

Chuggalug was getting tired, and realised that he couldn't outrun the two dinosaurs much longer. Glancing over his shoulder to see how close they were. He didn't see the tree root, tripped over it, and fell to the ground with a crash. Winded, he rolled forward, over and over, into a clearing in the trees.

He lay on the ground, trying to get his breath back. He closed his eyes and waited for the velociraptors to catch him.

Chuggalug had his eyes tightly shut. His heart was pounding. He wanted to hold his breath but was gasping for air.

He clenched his fists when he felt the warm breath on his neck. He was caught by the back of his shirt and lifted off the ground. He let out a yell. His heart beat faster and he started to struggle and kick, trying to break free. He twisted round to get a kick at the monster. He opened his eyes and was astonished at what he saw. It was not the velociraptor who was lifting him up, but a giant diplodocus. The huge beast lifted him high into the air and sat him among the topmost branches of a tall tree at the edge of the clearing.

Chuggalug was hugging the branch of the tree, and wondering what was going to happen next. He heard a low rumbling sound and realised it was coming from the diplodocus. As if in answer to the sound, a louder rumbling came from the forest far below.

He looked down into the clearing. The large head and long neck of first one, then another, then more and more of the giants emerged from the trees round the clearing.

Chuggalug had never seen a diplodocus before. Their long necks became thicker and thicker till they merged into gigantic speckled brown bodies, supported by four short muscular legs, like tree trunks. Their bodies then narrowed again and became tails, which were even longer than their necks, and he could hear the swishing of the air as the tails whipped back and forth.

Chuggalug was fascinated as he saw more and more of the giant animals appear from the forest, until the clearing round the tree was filled with a herd of the biggest moving things he had ever seen.

He watched, spellbound as some of the giants went to the river to drink. He even saw two of them pick up round pebbles from the river and swallow them. He remembered his dad telling him that some dinosaurs did this to help digest their food, but as he watched he screwed up his nose and thought it didn't look very tasty.

In the midst of all the dust thrown up by the herd as they milled about below, and the rumbling and snorting as they talked to each other, Chuggalug suddenly remembered the velociraptors.

The diplodocus, which had lifted him into the tree and was obviously the leader of the herd, swung its long neck up and looked right into his eyes. Chuggalug was startled. He pulled back, nearly losing his grip of the branch. Was this giant beast going to eat him? He was sure his dad had told him they only ate leaves.

What happened next made him smile with relief. As he looked into the enormous green eyes of the dinosaur, it gave him a huge wink. "Stay nice and quiet boy and you'll be alright with us." In that moment, Chuggalug knew that these giants were his friends and that they would look after him.

The two velociraptors crashed into the clearing and saw the herd of diplodocus.

Chuggalug heard the furious squeals and screeches of the velociraptors as they pranced about among the herd of diplodocus, standing up on their hind legs, as tall as they could, to try to find him. They looked really scary, and their screams

and roars made them even more so. He held on tightly to the tree and hoped that none of his new friends would get hurt.

"Hey you, stupid!" squealed the first one, prancing about to avoid being trampled on by the giant beasts

"Hey you, tiny brain!" called the second one, "we're talking to you. Have you seen a boy come through here? We're looking for a boy. Eh! Eh! Come on! Come on! We haven't all day. Have you seen a boy?"

The diplodocus turned slowly and looked down at the two velociraptors. "Dum de dum de dum... Boy?" said one, slowly. "Boy? Now what would that be then? Anybody know if we've seen a boy?"

"Dunno. What would a boy look like then? Oops! Sorry" said another as his huge tail whipped round and clattered one of the velociraptors on the head, knocking it head over heels across the clearing.

Chuggalug soon realised that, even to these fierce, fast and cunning killers, the diplodocus herd were giants, far too big to attack and too dangerous to get close to. His smile grew even wider as he watched the herd stamping around, knocking the velociraptors over, again and again, and making them angrier and angrier. He had to bite his lip to stop himself laughing out loud when the herd all started to swish their long tails like whips, making the velociraptors jump higher and higher to avoid being lashed or bowled over again.

"Aah! Get out of the way," yelled one, as it got to its feet and ducked to avoid another enormous tail as it swished over his head. "You lot are too stupid. Big and stupid! Big and stupid!" he shouted as they both bounded off into the forest to look for him, both screaming and snorting with rage.

The herd of diplodocus slowly became calm again. Chuggalug heard them rumbling and grunting quietly to one another and he was sure that the giants were chuckling together.

The leading diplodocus again swung his head up to look at Chuggalug. "Thank you," he said nervously. "My name is Chuggalug and I don't know what would have happened to me if you hadn't been here. Could you please help me down? I must get home and I don't know how far it is."

"You're welcome Chuggalug" said the diplodocus. "My name is Derandan and this is my herd. We don't like those velociraptors anyway, but more important, do you know your way home from here?"

"No I don't" said Chuggalug fearfully. "Could you help me down please?" The great dinosaur gently caught the back of his shirt again, and, instead of lowering him to the ground, lifted him even higher, far above the treetops. Chuggalug looked around and gave a whoop of joy when, in the distance, he spotted the tree house. He didn't have far to go, and he would soon be home safe and sound.

Derandan lowered him to the ground. "Thank you all very much," said Chuggalug. "I don't think you're stupid at all."

"Don't worry about that, Chuggalug," said Derandan. "Off you go home, and we'll keep an eye on you, and always remember, the loudest person, who calls everyone else stupid, is usually the stupidest one of all." He giggled as the herd jostled and pushed each other, and all tried to sniff him, or nudge him with their noses, all grunting and snorting quietly. It was a comforting, friendly sound. Chuggalug's new friends were the biggest a boy ever had.

The low rumbling and gentle grunting from the herd told Chuggalug that they understood, and as he skipped off along the riverbank towards home, leaving them grazing on the shoots and leaves high in the tree tops, or drinking from the clear waters of the river, he knew that he would see them again.

Chuggalug ran home and climbed up the rope ladder into the tree house. He ran to his bedroom and went to the window. He looked out over the forest and smiled when, in the distance, he spotted the heads of the diplodocus herd popping up above the tops of the trees. He heard them rumbling and mumbling to each other as they went. "Dum de dum de dum de dum" he smiled to himself and thought how different the diplodocus were to the way they appeared if you didn't know them. Just like people really.

Forest Fire

The pteranodon flew high above the great forest, which stretched out below him as far as he could see. He glided effortlessly, riding the rising currents of warm air. His enormous leathery wings flapped only occasionally and cast a giant shadow which sped across the green carpet of trees far below. His head, with its long pointed beak and huge bony crest, turned slowly from side to side as if he was searching for something on the ground.

He soared high above the mountains. He saw where the tiny stream started, and tumbled down the mountain on its way to join the mighty river, shimmering in the bright sunshine as it flowed on and on to the great sea, far away to the North.

He watched a great herd of iguanodon grazing on their favourite shrub, the white flowered protoanthus, in a large clearing in the distance. The white patch of shrubs stood out brightly in the seemingly endless green and brown of the forest.

He followed the glittering waters of the river further and further downstream, scanning the banks as he went. Suddenly he spotted what he was looking for.

In a clearing in the forest beside the river was a magnificent tall tree. High in the topmost branches, a tree house had been built, with a veranda, which looked out over the top of the forest.

By the side of the river, at the edge of the clearing, the pteranodon saw a boy with bright red hair playing alone. The great flying dinosaur circled slowly above the clearing, its eyes fixed on the boy as he played. Chuggalug played on, totally unaware that he was being watched from above.

The pteranodon circled lower and lower, silent save for the quiet hiss of air over his vast wings. He could now hear the gurgling of the water over the rocks, and the splashes as Chuggalug threw pebbles into the river.

Chuggalug had his arm raised to throw another pebble, but froze as the giant shadow flashed across the water in front of him. He looked up and saw the pteranodon above him. He started to run towards the tree house, but he was too late. The huge animal landed right in front of him, its enormous wings spread out, blocking the way. Chuggalug was trapped.

The boy and the pteranodon faced each other, neither of them moving. Chuggalug stared into the big green eyes of the pteranodon, watching for any sign that it was about to attack him. Then something amazing happened.

The pteranodon suddenly lowered its head to the ground in

front of Chuggalug, and flattened its great wings on the grass, in an obvious display of friendship. "Hello, Chuggalug. Don't you remember me?"

"N n no I don't" stammered Chuggalug, slowly backing away. Then he realised where he had seen the pteranadon before. "I remember" he shouted. "Your mum saved me when I fell over the cliff. She took me to her nest in the mountains. You were one of the babies in the nest."

"That's right" said the pteranadon. "My name is Toby, and I said I would visit you when I could fly, so here I am." Chuggalug jumped up and down with excitement, thinking of the brilliant adventures he could have with his new friend. He couldn't believe his ears when he heard Toby say "Climb on my back and hold on tight. Let's go flying and see what we can see."

Chuggalug climbed on and held on round Toby's neck, with his feet dangling below. Toby turned to face the slight breeze, spread his gigantic wings and waited.

When a gust of wind came, Toby took two steps and leapt into the air. Chuggalug gasped as he was carried up and up, above the treetops and high into the blue sky. "EEE HAA!" he squealed, as Toby dived down, skimming the trees and soared up again high above the forest. This was the best fun a boy could ever have.

Chuggalug felt the wind blowing through his hair and snatching at his face as they flew higher and higher. The forest, far below, stretched away into the distance as far as he could see. He saw the dark mountains far away. He tried to pick out the place in the mountains where his friend Boing Boing the sabre-toothed tiger lived in a cave, but it was too far away.

Chuggalug was still laughing and squealing with excitement when he saw Toby's head snap round. He had spotted something in the distance. Chuggalug followed Toby's gaze and saw the plume of white smoke rising from the forest. He felt a chill rising in his stomach. His dad had told him about forest fires, and how dangerous they were.

Toby turned and flew towards the smoke. Soon they could see the long line of yellow flames leaping up from the forest, marching along and leaving nothing but black smouldering stumps behind.

Then Chuggalug heard something which made his blood run cold.

In front of the flames he could hear the screeches, bellows and roars, as terrified animals tried to outrun the flames. Small raptors were racing along beside enormous stegosaurs with their huge bony plates along their backs. In front of them he saw a triceratops roaring with fear, its three great horns high in the air as it crashed along, oblivious to everything but the smoke and flames behind it.

As they flew low over the flames towards the front of the melee of fleeing dinosaurs Chuggalug gave a shout of fear. Right at the front was his friend Derandan, with the herd of diplodocus, lumbering along as fast as their huge bulk would let them, and sounding like a thunderstorm as they went, knocking over bushes and trees in their path. Chuggalug cried, "We've got to help them, Toby. It's Derandan and his herd."

Toby flew over the heads of the herd and rose up higher into the air. Chuggalug was even more horrified when he saw what was ahead. The

herd of panicking, terrified dinosaurs, with Derandan in front, was heading straight for a huge cliff, and certain death.

Suddenly Chuggalug spotted something, which gave him some hope. "Look Toby!" he yelled into the pteranodon's ear. "There's a gap in the flames behind them. They can't see it for the smoke. If we can get them to turn towards the flames they'll be safe."

"Fly down close to the leading diplodocus," shouted Chuggalug. "That's Derandan. I'll shout to him and tell him to turn. The rest of the herd will follow him".

Toby flew down low, and swooped over the rumbling herd of

diplodocus towards Derandan, right at the front. "Derandan! Turn round! There's a cliff ahead!" Chuggalug yelled at the top of his voice, as they flew over the huge dinosaur. But it was obvious that, amid the roaring of the forest fire and the rumbling of the herd of stampeding dinosaurs, Derandan couldn't hear Chuggalug's warning and lumbered on towards the cliff edge.

"It's no use!" Chuggalug shouted in Toby's ear. "He can't hear me. We'll have to fly over him again. I'll drop on to his neck and try to get him to turn the herd round."

Toby swooped down low over the herd of thundering, panicking giants as they raced clumsily towards the cliff edge, which was getting closer and closer.

Chuggalug could hear the huge beasts grunting, and saw their eyes rolling upwards with fear as they tried to outrun the smoke and flames. He prepared to drop.

Now Chuggalug was right above Derandan's head. He felt the thick smoke stinging his eyes and catching his throat, making him cough, and making it difficult to see how far he had to drop. He knew that if he missed Dandan he would fall to the ground in front of the stampeding herd of dinosaurs and in front of the forest fire. He let go of Toby's neck and dropped into the smoke.

He landed with a thump on Derandan's neck, just behind his head, and just in front of the row of jagged spines, which ran the length of the dinosaur's back, right to the tip of his tail. He held on as tightly as he could. The terrified beast, who couldn't see for the smoke, let out a roar when he felt Chuggalug landing on the back of his neck and started to shake his head in terror. Chuggalug felt his grip loosening and knew that he was about to be thrown to the ground, under the feet of the herd of giants lumbering along behind.

"Derandan, it's me, Chuggalug! You must turn round! There's a cliff in front and you're going straight for it!" Chuggalug yelled as loudly as he could. He saw Derandan's head twitch up and round as he recognised his voice. He saw the fear in the dinosaur's eyes and realised that he wasn't turning, but lumbering on towards the edge of the cliff, which was getting closer and closer.

"You must turn round" Chuggalug yelled again. This time he twisted Derandan's enormous head round to the left and pointed frantically towards the approaching flames. "You must trust me! There's a gap in the flames and it's our only hope."

Slowly, ever so slowly Chuggalug felt the gigantic dinosaur turn in the direction he was pointing. "Go on, Derandan!" he shouted, as he felt him hesitate, realising he was running towards the dreaded flames.

Chuggalug watched as the whole herd of diplodocus turned to follow their leader. Other dinosaurs also turned, blindly following the herd, away from the cliff and back towards the fire.

Chuggalug could hear the giant dinosaurs getting more and more frightened as they rumbled along behind, getting closer and closer to the huge wall of yellow flames. "Keep going! Keep going!" he shouted at the top of his voice, not sure if any of them heard him above the roar of the herd and the loud crackling of the flames.

Suddenly they were through the

flames and smoke and into the fresh air. The forest fire swept on to the cliffs and there it burned itself out.

The herd of dinosaurs gradually slowed down and stopped. Derandan lowered his head and Chuggalug dropped to the ground. Suddenly he was surrounded by diplodocus, all grunting and rumbling their thanks to him. He thought he was going to be tickled to death as the giant beasts jostled and pushed each other, all trying to lick him at the same time.

"That's okay," laughed Chuggalug. "You all saved me from the velociraptors and, anyway, you should also thank my friend Toby, the pteranodon. He helped me to save you."

The friendly rumbling and grunting increased when Toby landed beside Chuggalug and lowered his head for him to climb back on to his shoulders.

Chuggalug felt once more the thrill when Toby rose into the sky. He felt even better when he looked down and saw that hundreds of dinosaurs, of all shapes and sizes had followed the diplodocus herd through the gap in the flames and were now safe.

Toby and Chuggalug flew higher and higher above the forest, and followed the river, far below, back to the clearing with the tree house.

Toby landed on the grass, at the edge of the clearing and Chuggalug jumped down from his back. "Thank you for coming to see me" said Chuggalug. "I hope we can go flying again soon, but let's pick a day with no forest fires."

Toby spread his huge wings and rose into the sky. Chuggalug watched and waved until the pteranodon was just a speck in the blue sky. He then turned and walked slowly to the rope ladder, which took him up into the tree house, where he knew his mum would be making supper. What a story he had to tell her about his new friend Toby pteranadon.

Cousins

Chuggalug was playing in his boat. It wasn't a real boat; it was made of logs, tied together with vine ropes, but to Chuggalug it was the best boat in the world.

The boat was his secret. No one else in the whole world knew about it. He kept it in a secret place, hidden in thick bushes beside a large pool in the river, just downstream from the tree house clearing.

The sun was shining warm and bright in the blue sky. Chuggalug lay back on the boat, his hand trailing lazily in the water, dreaming about the games he would play later with his best friend Boing Boing the sabre-toothed tiger.

Far away in the distance, Chuggalug could hear the rumbles of a thunderstorm, somewhere over the dark mountains, too far away to bother him.

Chuggalug closed his eyes as the boat drifted slowly across the pool towards the other bank of the river. Sometimes he would hear the screech of a small animal, or the roar of a dinosaur deep in the forest, but it really felt very peaceful, lying in the boat, listening to the noises getting farther and farther away and quieter and quieter.

As Chuggalug slowly drifted off to sleep in the bottom of the boat, he was completely unaware of the rising waters. Fed by the storm, far off in the mountains, the river water turned brown and flowed deeper and deeper, faster and faster, carrying the boat, and Chuggalug, farther and farther away from the clearing and the tree house.

A sudden jolt, as the boat crashed into a large rock in the river, woke Chuggalug with a start. Confused and frightened, he sat up and looked round.

The boat was rushing along in the fast flowing floodwater, rocking from side to side, and being turned round and round, so that Chuggalug had to hold on tightly to the sides to stop himself being thrown out into the deep dark waters.

Chuggalug was very frightened. He shouted and shouted for help as loudly as he could, but he knew that the roaring and rumbling of the river water was far too loud for anyone to hear his cries.

It was then that Chuggalug realised that the current carrying the boat was getting stronger, and that the roaring of the water ahead was getting louder. He looked downstream and was horrified by what he saw. An enormous plume of white spray rose above the river ahead, and Chuggalug knew that he was being swept towards a huge waterfall.

Chuggalug held on to the sides of the boat as tightly as he could and stared in horror as the tiny collection of branches and rope rushed headlong towards the waterfall. Faster and faster, nearer and nearer to the roaring torrent of water.

Then Chuggalug decided to jump. He leapt from the boat into the foaming frothing water and swam as fast as he could towards the riverbank. The boat rushed on, over the lip of the waterfall, falling and tumbling down and down, smashing into a thousand pieces as it crashed on the rocks far below.

Chuggalug was swimming as hard as he could. He was getting closer to the riverbank, but he knew that he was also being swept in the direction of the waterfall. He was almost exhausted, when he felt his hand touch something. He grabbed hold and realised that he had caught the end of a tree branch, which was trailing in the water. He grabbed the branch with both hands and held on as tightly as he could, all the time feeling the raging river sucking and pulling him towards the waterfall.

Chuggalug used all his strength to pull himself slowly up, one hand at a time, towards the thicker part of the branch and the safety of the riverbank. His arms were aching, his hands were cold and sore, but he was gradually getting closer to the water's edge. He could see a thick tree root on the bank, just above the surface of the water, and he knew that if he could grab hold of it he might be able

to pull himself out of the water on to the bank.

He tensed himself, ready to make a lunge for the tree root and gave a last pull on the branch to help him. Horrified, Chuggalug heard the loud crack as the branch he had been holding gave up its struggle with the brown bubbling floodwater and broke, throwing him back into the river, tumbling upside down and round about and out into space, over the edge of the waterfall.

Screaming and yelling, Chuggalug felt himself falling and falling, faster and faster towards the boiling frothing pool and the dark jagged rocks far below, He closed his eyes and curled himself up into a ball.

Suddenly he was under water, being sucked down by the swirling torrent, deeper and deeper.

He held his breath and tried to swim upwards towards the surface and the fresh air. Just when he thought his lungs would burst, he felt the warm air on his face as he reached the surface, and found himself at the edge of the pool. He grabbed hold of a large rock at the water's edge, pulled himself out of the water and lay on his back on the pebbles, gasping for air.

As he lay there on his back, he could see the water rushing over the edge of the cliff, high above him, and down to roar into the dark pool beside him. He just couldn't believe that he had fallen over the waterfall and was lying there, tired, cold, wet and frightened, but unhurt.

Chuggalug lay there on his back for ages, fascinated by the sight of the water plunging, seemingly in slow motion, over the cliff and roaring into the deep, dark pool beside him.

After a while he sat up and looked round about, trying to work out how he was going to get home. The cliffs seemed to loom high above him as far as he could see in both directions. Chuggalug realised that the only way back was to climb up the cliff, beside the waterfall, and follow the river back to the clearing, the tree house, and his Mum and Dad.

Chuggalug was very frightened.

He got up and scrambled over the rocks, round the pool to the bottom of the huge cliff. He took a deep breath and started to climb, finding little cracks and ledges in the rock of the cliff for his hands and feet, slowly edging himself up, higher and higher, all the time being sprayed by the water as it splashed on the rock face on its way down the waterfall.

He seemed to have been climbing forever, scared to look down at the dark pool and the rocks far below, and unable to look up with the tumbling water splashing into his face and his eyes. He knew he was becoming exhausted, and his hands and feet were getting cold and numb. He slowly realised that he could not climb any further. He held himself flat against the cliff, pressing his cheek against the cold, wet rock, trying to work out what he could do.

Chuggalug felt his cold hands slowly slipping, and losing their grip on the rock.

He knew that he was going to fall at any moment, down towards the rocks far below, and he knew that there was nothing he could do to prevent it. He felt his fingertips slowly sliding on the cold, wet, rough rock. Chuggalug tensed himself ready for the long plunge down the cliff.

Then a movement in the waterfall caught his eye.

It was something white in the water of the waterfall. He screwed up his eyes and shook the water out of them to see better. His eyes opened wide with amazement as a wet hand reached out to him from the waterfall. He caught hold of it and felt himself being gently pulled into the waterfall, along a ledge which was getting wider and wider. The water was falling heavier and stronger on his head as he edged his way along the ledge, making it hard to breathe and forcing him to shut his eyes. Then suddenly he was through the waterfall and standing behind it. He opened his eyes. He was at the mouth of a great dark cave with the waterfall tumbling down like a great hissing curtain behind him.

Chuggalug slowly realised that he was still holding tightly to the hand that had guided him through the waterfall. He looked up and standing in front of him was a girl about the same age as himself, with long red hair and a smiling face. She was watching him curiously with her head tilted slightly to one side as his hand still gripped hers tightly as if it was frightened to let go.

"Are you all right?" she asked quietly.

"YYYes I think so," said Chuggalug slowly "but I'm not sure yet where I am, or how I got here."

"This is my secret place," said the girl "I love to come here and watch the water, but this is the first time I've ever seen a boy going down the waterfall."

"I didn't mean to go over the waterfall!" said Chuggalug, and told the girl all about his boat and how he came to plunge over the cliff into the pool.

"My name is Fern. What's yours?" asked the girl. "My name is Chuggalug," he replied "and thank you for saving me. I would certainly have fallen back down the cliff if you hadn't."

"My dad told me I have a cousin called Chuggalug," said Fern. "He lives with his mum and dad in a tree house in the forest, but I've never met him."

"That's me!" said Chuggalug excitedly, "and you must be my cousin Fern. My mum and dad told me I had a cousin who lived in a cave, but I never thought that the first time I met her she would save my life."

"Let's go," said Fern. "I'll take you to meet my mum and dad."

They set off through the cave with Fern leading the way. Chuggalug was a bit nervous and held on to Fern's hand until his eyes adjusted to the dim light in the cave, which were lit only by thin shafts of light from cracks in the rock letting in sunlight from above.

Once his eyes adjusted to the light, however, Chuggalug was amazed at the sight of the magical, majestic caverns he was walking through, some with great lakes of dark still water, and all with walls speckled with sparkling pebbles and crystals.

Chuggalug thought it was a beautiful place.

"Here we are" shouted Fern as she skipped into another cavern. This one was different. It was lit by the flames of torches flickering round the walls. A big fire was burning in the corner, with the smoke rising up into a large chimney in the roof. The floor was scattered with fur rugs and the whole cave felt lovely and warm. At the back of the cave the flickering flames of the torches were reflected in the black surface of an underground river.

"Here's my mum and dad" called Fern as she ran across the cave to where a man and woman were sitting near the fire. "This is my cousin

Chuggalug" she squealed excitedly as her mum and dad stood up.

"Hello, Chuggalug" said Fern's dad. "How did you get here?"

"You're soaking wet," said Fern's mum, as Chuggalug started his story of the boat, the waterfall and the cliff. "Come over to the fire and get warm and dry, while I get you some food."

When Chuggalug had told his tale and was dry and warm again, Fern's dad stood up. "Let's get you home then, young man, before it gets dark."

"Can I come too, dad?" shouted Fern, jumping up and down with excitement. "You said you would take me to see the tree house one day. Can I, can I please?"

"Okay" said Fern's dad, laughing. "We'll all go."

Chuggalug and Fern giggled and laughed as they skipped out of the cave into the forest on their way to the clearing in the forest and the tree house where Chuggalug lived with his mum and dad. On the way he told her about Boing Boing, the sabre-toothed tiger, and the dinosaurs who had become his friends.

Chuggalug and Fern were so happy and excited at the thought of all the games and adventures they could have together in the land of the dinosaurs.

Four New Friends

Chuggalug was very excited. His mum and dad had given him permission to visit Boing Boing's cave at the foot of the great mountains, and as Fern and her mum and dad were still staying with them in the tree house, she was to be allowed to accompany him.

The mountains were far away from the tree house. Chuggalug and Fern were really looking forward to their adventure, and were scampering about in the clearing waiting for Boing Boing.

Fern had never met Boing Boing and, though she would never admit it, she was feeling a little nervous about getting really close to a huge sabre-toothed tiger. Then, from the forest, she heard the loudest roar she had ever heard. She looked round and saw Boing Boing emerge from the forest. He was even bigger and fiercer looking than she had imagined.

The huge animal padded across the clearing towards them. The two enormous tusks hanging from his mouth glinted in the sunshine. Fern tried to be brave and not run away. Then Chuggalug caught her hand "Come on, Fern" he yelled. "Come and meet Boing Boing" pulling her eagerly towards the tiger.

Reaching Boing Boing, Chuggalug threw himself at the tiger and hugged him. Fern was still a bit nervous, but when the great beast lay down on the grass in front of her, gave a deep purr and stretched out his enormous paw towards her, her fear disappeared and she joined Chuggalug in hugging Boing Boing.

"This is my cousin Fern" said Chuggalug. "Is it okay if she comes to your cave with us? Please say it is. She'd love to meet the cubs." When Boing Boing turned his huge head and gave Fern's face a great sloppy lick, they knew it was okay and both squealed and jumped up and down with excitement.

Chuggalug had been to the cave before, when the four cubs were born, and had asked Boing Boing to take him back to see them again, before they became fully-grown, and left the cave as adult sabre-toothed tigers, to find their own dens in the forest.

Chuggalug and Fern climbed on to Boing Boing's back and waved to their mums and dads as the big tiger set off through the forest towards the mountains far away. They held on tightly to the soft thick fur as they bounded along, laughing, and shouting "Boing! Boing! Boing!" in time to the tiger's steps.

Fern thought it was wonderful being in the forest with Boing Boing. She could hear the roars and crashes of great dinosaurs nearby but she wasn't afraid, although she did sometimes find herself holding on to

Boing Boing a little bit tighter.

It seemed ages before they reached the edge of the forest, where the trees thinned out and the mountains loomed ahead, dark and dangerous. At last they spotted the cave entrance.

With a whoop of excitement, Chuggalug jumped down from Boing Boing's back. He started running towards the cave but was suddenly knocked on his back by an avalanche of yellow and black fur as the four cubs raced out of the cave to meet him. They squealed in welcome and licked and licked at his face till he was sore with laughing and begged them to stop.

He sat up in the middle of the

circle of tiger cubs and looked around at them. "Fern, come and meet the cubs." She had been standing watching the rough and tumble, smiling. She then sat down beside Chuggalug and giggled when one of the cubs crawled forward and laid his warm furry head on her lap.

He couldn't believe how big they had grown. They were almost as big as Boing Boing, and their mum growled a warning to them to be careful as they playfully thumped Chuggalug with their big furry paws, knocking him over in their excitement

"Hi, you lot," giggled Chuggalug, "Sit still a minute till I tell Fern your names."

He looked at them all carefully.

"This is Tim. He's the biggest."

"This is Tom. He's the smallest."

"This is Tam. He's the fastest."

"And the one with his head on your lap is Tum. He's the chubbiest."

"Tim, Tom, Tam and Tum the tigers" laughed Fern. "What cool names."

"Let's play a game," shouted Chuggalug.

The cubs all jumped up and dived on Chuggalug, rolling over in a bundle of growling, purring fur, all pretending to chew bits of each other, or bits of Chuggalug. Fern laughed and laughed at this fierce looking struggle, then decided to dive in and join it.

After a while the struggle

subsided and they all lay panting on the grass. "Right," said Chuggalug "Let's play the chasing game. Fern and I shall run off into the forest and you lot try to find us."

The four cubs grunted in agreement and all turned their back to the forest and waited, so that Chuggalug and Fern could run off and hide.

The four tiger cubs were eager to give chase, but decided to wait a few minutes to give Chuggalug and Fern a chance to get away.

The two children ran and ran through the forest, as fast as their legs would carry them, laughing and giggling at the thought of the four cubs chasing them.

They had run for ages, sometimes glancing over their shoulders and listening for the cubs behind them. Chuggalug was just in front and was running between two trees when he suddenly tripped over the log.

Fern jumped the log and ran to Chuggalug who had tumbled into a pile of leaves. "Are you okay?" she asked anxiously. "I'm fine. Don't worry." He stood up, laughing and brushing the leaves off with his hands.

Then a movement caught Chuggalug's eye. He looked between the trees and was horrified to see the log, which he had tripped over, slowly start to move. Chuggalug realised that it wasn't a log, and stopped laughing. He caught Fern's arm and slowly pulled her towards the edge of the clearing. "Chuggalug, what is it? What's wrong?" whispered Fern. He nodded towards the movement at the forest edge. Fern followed his stare and froze.

The "log" was the tail of a velociraptor, which had been sleeping. The dinosaur leapt to its feet and studied the two children carefully. Slowly it advanced into the clearing, perfectly balanced and ready to pounce at any time. It dawned on Chuggalug that he had seen this monster before. It was one of the two, which had chased him when the diplodocus herd had saved him. But there were no giant helpers here now. Staring into the unblinking yellow eyes, Chuggalug knew that they couldn't outrun it, and they were on their own.

"I know you," hissed the velociraptor slowly and menacingly. "You escaped the last time we chased you. I think those big, stupid long necked diplodocus helped you… but they're not here to help you now, boy." All the time he was talking, the velociraptor was slowly circling Chuggalug and Fern, ready to pounce at any moment.

Chuggalug and Fern held their breath as the dinosaur crouched. They stood perfectly still. The dinosaur's short muscular tail rose up behind it as it prepared to leap. Then Tam arrived.

Chuggalug and Fern both jumped at the sudden explosion of twigs, branches, leaves and black and yellow fur as the tiger cub crashed into the clearing and bombed into the crouching dinosaur, knocking it over and landing on top of it.

The monster leapt to its feet, roaring, screaming and spitting with fury. Tam got up, scampered over beside the two open-mouthed children, and stood facing the velociraptor, trying to look fierce.

The furious velociraptor, angrily snorting and growling, advanced slowly and menacingly towards Chuggalug, Fern and Tam.

Chuggalug and Fern were still very scared, but giggled at the sight of the Velociraptor's face when Tom and Tim arrived into the clearing, at the same breakneck speed as Tam had, and both crashed into the dinosaur, which was again sent flying, this time battering his head into a tree.

He got up again, trying to look angry and fierce, but the children could only laugh as the dinosaur staggered around the clearing trying not to fall over. The dinosaur's final straw came in the shape of Tum, who arrived last into the clearing. He was so busy looking at Chuggalug and Fern that he didn't even see the velociraptor, charged right into it and sent it flying into the air, into the middle of an enormous thorn bush.

The monster squealed with pain and jumped high into the air as the thorns stuck into him. He ran off into the forest roaring and squealing, thinking he had been attacked by a herd of sabre-toothed tigers. Chuggalug, Fern and the four cubs rolled about on the ground squealing and laughing as the roars and crashes of the dinosaur became quieter and quieter as it ran farther and farther away.

The six youngsters were still giggling and laughing about their adventure when they got back to the cave where Boing Boing was waiting to take Chuggalug and Fern home.

The children waved as they

climbed on Boing Boing's back. "Goodbye, Tim. Goodbye, Tom. Goodbye, Tam. Goodbye, Tum" they called as Boing Boing set off.

The four cubs raced round and round their dad as he padded off towards the forest, until a loud roar from their mum summoned them back to the cave.

Chuggalug and Fern waved and watched as the four bundles of fur disappeared. They held on tight as the huge tiger took them back through the forest to the tree house. What a story they had to tell when they got home.

Danger in the Caves

"Come on, Chuggalug!" Fern was skipping on in front and was getting impatient. Chuggalug was wandering along, his mouth open in wonder as he took in the beauty of the magnificent cavern. He held his burning torch high. It was a long stick with the end wrapped with skins and soaked in tar. The bright yellow flame lit up the cavern and he marvelled at the glittering crystals, which were like stars in the high dark roof.

A lake of black still water seemed to fill the cavern. They were walking along a narrow beach of small round multicoloured pebbles. Chuggalug couldn't resist the

temptation to stop and throw a pebble into the water. He smiled as he heard the "plop". He gasped as he saw the reflection of the flame in the ripples cast huge expanding circles of light on the sparkling dark ceiling high above.

"Chuggalug. Come on!" Fern lived in the caves and had seen it all before. Chuggalug hadn't and was spellbound. He was used to the tree house and the endless sky. The caves were deep and dark, and Chuggalug found exploring them exciting, and a little bit scary.

Just like in the forest, there were places in the caves where it was safe to play, and places where Chuggalug and Fern weren't supposed to go, but just like in the forest, sometimes they were so engrossed in what they were doing that they forgot. This was one of those times.

They had discovered an underground stream, and had been following it for ages as it tumbled over the rocks, and wound its way through the caves. Suddenly the cave had opened up into this huge dark cavern, and the stream lost itself in the enormous underground lake.

"Look, Fern" called Chuggalug, pointing to the reflections high above them. He squealed with delight when he heard his voice echo round the cavern. Fern joined in and they both squealed again and again as they heard their voices echoing from the other end of the cavern, far off and invisible in the darkness, beyond the light of the torches.

Sticking the torches into the pebbles at the water's edge, they both picked up handfuls of the small, round stones and started throwing them into the water, fascinated by the way the ripples reflected the light from the torches into waves of light, flowing across the roof of the cavern, high above.

"I think we'd better go back now" said Fern after a few minutes, realising that they were in a strange part of the caves. "Just a few more minutes," laughed Chuggalug, who was having such fun. "We only have to follow the stream back to where we started, and the torches will burn for ages yet."

"Okay" said Fern, "but we must go soon." She sat down and started to collect some of the shiniest, prettiest pebbles to take home to her mum.

Chuggalug was crawling about on his hands and knees, looking for the flattest, roundest stones to skim, when suddenly he seemed to be pushed over and landed on his side. He looked round and saw Fern sitting on the stones next to him.

"Don't do that!" he shouted, laughing.

He then saw that Fern was not laughing, and that she was looking a bit frightened. "I didn't do anything," said Fern, slowly. "The ground moved. That's what made us fall."

Chuggalug was just about to tell Fern not to be silly, that the ground didn't move, when he felt it, and heard it. The ground was moving under his hands and knees, and he could hear a deep rumbling sound, which seemed to fill the whole of the huge cavern.

Chuggalug jumped to his feet and tried to run towards the two burning torches that they had stuck into the pebbles of the beach, when the ground shook again and he fell on his front at the same time as the torches fell into the lake and spluttered out. The cavern was plunged into complete darkness.

"Don't move!" said Chuggalug, trying not to sound frightened, which was very difficult, since he couldn't see anything at all, not even the pebbles in front of his face. He tried moving his hand right in front of his eyes but even touching his face he could see nothing, it was so dark.

"Where are you?" he whispered. "I'll crawl towards you."

"I'm here, right beside you," said Fern, startling Chuggalug, who hadn't realised she was so close. "What happened? What made the ground move like that?"

"I think it was an earthquake," said Chuggalug. "My dad told me about them and they can be very dangerous. We have to get out of here in case it happens again, but I don't know how we're going to find our way in this darkness."

"We must hold hands, so we don't get separated," said Fern. "The pebble beach is sloping into the lake, so if we walk back, with the lake to our right, we'll come to the entrance where the river comes in."

"Yes! Great!" said Chuggalug. "But be very careful, we don't want to fall in the water."

They started to make their way, slowly and cautiously, back the way they had come, feeling their way with their feet, in case they fell over a rock or into a hole in the pitch darkness.

They shouted for help, as loudly as they could, but their shouts echoed back at them louder than ever, until they seemed to fill the whole cavern with noise. It was so loud that they both stopped shouting and stumbled along in silence, holding hands tightly.

All of a sudden Chuggalug walked into the wall of the cavern with a bump and fell back with a crash, onto his bottom. "Are you okay?" asked Fern anxiously.

"Yes," answered Chuggalug "I must have strayed away from the edge of the lake and walked into the wall. I'll try to be more careful."

"Chuggalug, you didn't stray away from the edge of the lake," said Fern quietly. "I can feel the water with my foot. This is where the entrance should be. It must have been blocked by the earthquake."

"Oh no!" groaned Chuggalug as

he felt the solid wall of rock in front of them. "We'll have to find another way out. We must find the place where the river leaves the cavern and try to get out that way." They turned around and picked their way slowly back along the lakeside in the darkness.

They seemed to have been walking forever. Chuggalug had his free hand held out in front of him in case he walked into another solid wall. His arm was getting tired and he strained his eyes to try to see where he was going. He slowly realised that he could see the dark shape of his hand in front of him.

"It's getting lighter!" he shouted, excitedly. "I can see my hand!"

"Yes!" squealed Fern "I can see you. There must be light ahead. Let's go!"

They were walking quicker now, but had only gone a few steps when they stopped dead in their tracks. A deafening, deep, animal roar shook the cave in front of them and made them clutch each other's hand tighter. "What can that be?" whispered Fern. "It's coming towards us."

They crouched down quietly, straining their eyes to see what kind of monster was in the cave. The invisible beast roared again, closer and louder than before. The air in the cave seemed to shake with the noise.

Fern was astonished when Chuggalug suddenly started jumping

up and down, waving his arms and shouting, "We're here! We're here!" She caught his arm and pulled him back down. "What are you doing?" she hissed at him. "Be quiet! The monster will hear you."

"It's not a monster," called Chuggalug, stumbling forwards in the dark cave. "It's Boing Boing. Come on! He'll get us out of here!" Fern could hardly believe her eyes when she saw the shape of the huge sabre-toothed tiger picking its way carefully through the cave towards them. She laughed when Chuggalug threw his arms round its neck and gave it a huge hug.

Fern ran forward and hugged Boing Boing. "Thank goodness

you've found us. Let's get out of here before there's another earthquake."

Boing Boing lay down and they both climbed on to his broad furry back. They set off back through the cave and were soon out into the bright sunshine and heading for the cave where Fern lived with her mum and dad.

When they arrived at the mouth of the cave the two children jumped down from Boing Boing's back and hugged the big tiger again. Fern's mum and dad were very happy indeed to see them both safe and sound and waved gratefully to Boing Boing as he padded off into the forest. They seemed so happy that Chuggalug and Fern began to think that they wouldn't get into trouble for wandering off into the caves. Not yet, anyway.

Elgin

It was a strange sight. Chuggalug sat on the riverbank in the warm sunshine, his feet dangling in the cool clear water, now and then throwing a pebble into the pool, watching the splash and the ripples spreading out across the shimmering surface. It was not the boy, with his untidy mop of red hair, who made the sight strange. It was his companion. Lying stretched out beside him, fast asleep on the grass, was Chuggalug's best friend, Boing Boing, a magnificent sabre-toothed tiger, his head resting on his front paws, his huge sabre teeth glinting in the bright sunshine.

Chuggalug didn't hear the

people approaching through the forest. He saw Boing Boing's ears twitch and prick up, as the sleeping tiger sensed possible danger.

Chuggalug looked up and waved to his mum, who was watching him from the window of the tree house.

His gaze strayed down from the tree house and on to the sleeping tiger beside him. He leaned over and rested his head on the huge animal's warm, furry shoulder. Chuggalug thought he was the luckiest boy in the world to have a best friend like Boing Boing, and even though he knew that there were many fierce and dangerous dinosaurs wandering the forest, he always felt safe with the huge tiger by his side.

A movement in the trees at the edge of the clearing caught his eye and Chuggalug jumped to his feet. He whooped with delight when he recognised his cousin Fern and her mum and dad walking into the clearing. Fern ran on in front of her parents, laughing as she reached Chuggalug, falling on Boing Boing's back and giving the big tiger a huge hug. She giggled even more when Boing Boing turned his head and licked her face, for the tiger's enormous wet tongue was tickly.

Fern sat down on the riverbank beside Chuggalug and Boing Boing, chattering excitedly about their visit. They would be staying for a few days, so there would be plenty of time for lots of games, adventures and exploring.

When Chuggalug, eventually, managed to get a word in, he told Fern about his new boat. His dad had built it for him when his last one, which he had made himself, had been wrecked crashing over the waterfall downstream from the clearing. His dad had also told him that there was a fork in the river, before the waterfall, and if you took the right fork, it flowed safely on, beyond the waterfall and into the majestic River Spey.

It seemed to both Fern and Chuggalug that this was an adventure waiting for them, and they were soon busily loading the boat with food and water, just like real explorers. Unlike real explorers, however, they didn't tell anyone what they were doing or where they were going. Grown ups usually made such a fuss and might even stop them from going on their adventure. No. Best to say nothing.

Boing Boing watched anxiously as Chuggalug and Fern pushed off in the boat, out into the middle of the river and set off downstream on their great adventure.

They lazily drifted downstream, lying back in the boat, enjoying the warm sun on their faces and listening to the grunts and snorts of small animals rooting for food on the river banks. Occasionally the distant rumble or roar of much much larger creatures would remind them of the dangers hidden deep in the forest, all around.

A deep thundering sound in the distance made Chuggalug sit up. It was the sound of the waterfall ahead. Smiling to hide his slight fearfulness, he picked up the paddle from the bottom of the boat and prepared to steer them down the right fork in the river, safely past the huge drop of the falls.

The rumbling of the river plunging over the waterfall was becoming louder and louder. Chuggalug and Fern were sitting up in the boat now, and could see the large plume of white spray above the cataract just ahead. The boat was picking up speed when, to their relief, they spotted the entrance to the river branch to the right. Chuggalug paddled as hard as he could, and they both laughed as they entered the slower, calmer waters. There was a touch of nervousness and excitement in their laughter, as neither of them had ever been on this part of the river before. New adventures, perhaps dangers, lay ahead.

On and on they drifted, so excited about the adventure and the sights and sounds of the river that they were totally unaware of how far they had gone, and never gave a thought as to how to get back home.

Sometimes the river was narrow and fast flowing, sometimes wide, calm and slow.

Then Chuggalug spotted something he had never seen before. Just ahead, the river banks disappeared and the whole world seemed to be nothing but water as far as the eye could see. They both stared in amazement as the tiny boat left the land behind and started to bob around in the water, which was getting rather choppy.

"I know what this is," said Fern quietly. "It's the sea. I've heard my dad speak about it. It's where the river ends, and it goes on for ever. We have to get back to the land!" They lifted the two small wooden paddles and as hard as they could, splashed their way back towards the beach.

The waves seemed to be helping

them and they soon reached the shore. Jumping into the water, they dragged the boat up out of the water and lay down exhausted on the warm sand. After a few moments they both heard it at the same time. "Hey! You two on the shore! Over here!"

They looked out to sea again and saw a small island of sand just off the beach. The water seemed to be rising around it, and the island was getting smaller and smaller. On the island, and scurrying around in a very agitated fashion was a small dinosaur. "Hey! You two!" he called out again "Over here! Get me back to the land before this sand disappears altogether."

Chuggalug and Fern laughed

and jumped up. They pushed the boat back into the water and out to the small island, which was not very far off the beach. The small dinosaur jumped into the boat and they soon pushed it back to shore.

Back on dry land they studied the small creature. It was nearly up to Chuggalug's waist, had a collar of spikes round the back of its head, two rather fierce looking horns, a short stumpy tail and the friendliest face Chuggalug and Fern had ever seen.

"Hello," said Chuggalug. "Who are you? And how did you get stuck out there?"

The small dinosaur stood as tall as he could, and in a rather haughty voice announced "I am Elginia

Mirabilis, and I fell asleep on the sand and woke up to find myself surrounded by water. I don't like to get my feet wet, so I called you two over to get me back to land."

Chuggalug and Fern laughed at the small creature trying to look fierce, but not really succeeding. "Let's get you back to the rest of your family" said Fern. They saw a rather sad look come over Elginia's face. "There's no-one but me left. They've all gone. There were fewer and fewer and now there's only me, so I'll just come with you two. You look as if you need someone to look after you."

"Okay," laughed Chuggalug, "you can come back with us. I've already got Boing Boing to look after

me, but you can look after Fern."

"Oh yes!" squealed Fern with delight. "But Elginia Mirabilis is too big a name for such a small dinosaur. We'll call you Elgin for short."

They set off back along the river towards the forest and home. As they walked, Elgin looked back to the place where the river met the sea, and where he had lived till now. As he turned away with his new friends he had no idea that one day, far into the future, a handsome town, bearing his name, would be built there, and that, in that town, a fine museum would have a model of him as its prize exhibit, to be admired by many children.

Back Home

Chuggalug, Fern and Elgin made their way back along the riverbank, heading upstream, away from the sea and back towards the forest, the tree house and home. Chuggalug didn't say anything, but he knew that it would be a far more dangerous journey than the one downstream, when they were on the boat in the middle of the river, safe from any hungry or dangerous beast that might be in the area.

Fern, on the other hand, was happily skipping along beside her new best friend, Elgin, who also seemed to be very happy to be with them and no longer on his own. Fern had discovered that, although Elgin was not very big, he was really really strong, with short thick powerful legs and a broad back. To Fern's delight, this meant that she could sit on his back and he could easily carry her along, which was great fun for her, and made Elgin feel very happy.

After walking for ages in the warm sunshine, they decided to rest for a while. They picked some delicious blackberries and lay down on the river bank. Chuggalug felt his eyelids getting heavier and heavier, heard the whistling and chirping of the birds drifting farther and farther away, and was soon fast asleep.

He woke with a start. Someone was shouting. It was Fern. Where was she? She was shouting for help. He rubbed his eyes hard and looked round. Fern was sitting against a tree waving to him, with Elgin snorting and worriedly looking down at her. Chuggalug jumped up and ran over. "What happened?" he asked anxiously. "I caught my foot in a tree root," said Fern, obviously in pain. "I fell over and twisted my ankle. I can't stand on it. It's too painful. How are we going to get home if I can't walk?"

At this point, Elgin strutted over, with his head held high, and a twinkle in his eye. "It's no problem," he said. "You can sit on my back and I'll carry you. I knew you two would need me to look after you."

"He's right," said Chuggalug, laughing. "We'll get you to the river's edge and bathe your ankle in the cold water, and then Elgin can carry you home."

"Okay," said Fern, smiling at the sight of Elgin looking so proud. "Let's do it."

She put her arm round Chuggalug's shoulder, hopped to the bank of the river and sat down with her feet in the cool clear water, feeling the pain ease away. As they sat on the peaceful sunny riverbank, all three heard the roar at the same time. "What was that?" whispered Fern.

"I don't know, but it sounds huge, and not very friendly" replied Chuggalug, listening carefully, and anxiously scanning all round. Elgin had jumped up, and was also looking all round, sniffing the air, looking very agitated.

Once again a roar filled the air, this time much louder and much closer. They also heard the crunching and snapping as something very big crashed its way through the trees and shrubs, towards the river. "This must be a watering hole for the dinosaurs!" shouted Chuggalug. "And something very big is coming for a drink. We have to get out of here – now!"

Chuggalug caught Fern's hand to pull her up. She tried to stand, but winced with the pain of her injured ankle. Chuggalug was just trying to help her up on to Elgin's back when the roaring and crashing behind them made them look round. They all knew then that it was too late. They couldn't get away. Allosaurus, the biggest, fiercest dinosaur around, was standing at the edge of the clearing, curiously watching them, its huge head tilting from side to side as if it was trying to puzzle out what they were, its small, cold, black eyes flitting from one to the other, a long, deep grunting noise coming from somewhere deep in its insides, its enormous mouth slightly open, revealing rows of huge sharp teeth.

What happened next took Chuggalug, Fern, and allosaurus completely by surprise. Instead of running away, Elgin gave out his deepest roar and galloped straight at the massive dinosaur. "Run!" he shouted at Chuggalug and Fern as he scampered towards the beast. Chuggalug helped Fern along as she painfully tried to limp away. Allosaurus looked confused and lumbered towards them with a loud roar.

Then to their amazement and to allosaurus's complete shock, Elgin reappeared behind the huge beast, and appeared to scamper up its tail and onto its back. He sunk his sharp claws and teeth into its back, just behind its head and hung on tightly. The enormous dinosaur roared with fury and desperately tried to dislodge this horrible stinging little thing from its back. It couldn't reach Elgin with its razor-sharp front claws. It spun

round and round in an effort to throw him off, but the little dinosaur hung on tightly, and was still firmly fixed to its back when the huge beast thundered off, away towards the forest, roaring with anger and pain.

Chuggalug and Fern slowly made their way along the river-bank as far as they could until it became all quiet again and, exhausted, they sat down to rest. They both felt a bit tearful at the thought of what Elgin had done. They knew he had saved their lives, and were very worried about what had happened to him, and really sad thinking they might never see the brave little dinosaur again.

They both sat staring sadly into the sparkling water quietly thinking about brave little Elgin who had been their friend for so short a time.

"Can we go now?"

They nearly jumped out of their skins when Elgin's head appeared between them, looking from one to the other.

"Elgin!" shrieked Fern, jumping up and hugging him, completely forgetting the pain in her ankle. "What happened? How did you get away? You saved our lives! You're the best!" She held on tightly as she and Chuggalug listened to Elgin.

"Look," said the little dinosaur, matter-of-factly "It was only an allosaurus. They may be enormous, very fierce and a bit blood thirsty, but they're really quite stupid. I simply hung on till he ran into a part of the forest where the trees were so thick I knew he couldn't turn round, and then dropped of and ran back the other way. He was so pleased to be rid of me that he didn't bother chasing me. So here we are. Let's get you on my back, Fern, and be on our way before he does decide to come back for a drink."

Chuggalug helped Fern up on to Elgin's back and they set off, at a good pace, on up river towards home. Chuggalug led the way and little Elgin ambled proudly along behind, head held high and glancing round every now and then, to make sure Fern was okay up there on his broad back.

After a while Chuggalug heard a familiar sound. Away in the distance a steady rumble could be heard. "Listen!" he shouted excitedly. "Listen! It's the waterfall! We're nearly there!" Then a loud and very fierce sounding roar from up ahead made Elgin tense up and stop dead. "You two get behind me," he ordered. "I'll deal with this."

To his alarm and amazement Chuggalug didn't do what he said, but laughed and skipped on ahead, towards the danger. A huge sabre-toothed tiger appeared on the path ahead, and to Elgin's bewilderment, Chuggalug ran straight to it and gave it a great big hug.

"Elgin, come and meet Boing

Boing," shouted Chuggalug. "He's my best friend in the whole world. Boing Boing, this is Elgin. He saved our lives and carried Fern home. He's going to be Fern's friend like you are to me."

Just then, Chuggalug's mum and dad, and Fern's mum and dad appeared on the path. "We heard all that," said Chuggalug's dad with a happy smile. "Welcome, little fellow," he said, patting Elgin on the snout. "Now let's get home, and get some food. You all look exhausted."

They all made their way back to the clearing in the forest. Fern's mum and dad fussed around her, hearing how she had injured her ankle and again and again, how brave little Elgin had saved them from allosaurus.

Chuggalug and Fern had a feeling, deep down, that very soon they would have to explain how they came to have such an adventure so far from home, but that would come later. For now they would enjoy being home safely, and welcoming Elgin to the forest.

The Gift

Chuggalug had a problem. It was coming up to Fern's birthday, and he didn't have a present to give her. She had given him a beautiful bow and arrows that her dad had made for him, and he loved playing with them, shooting the arrows as far as he could across the clearing. He was getting better and better, and could fire the arrows right across from one side of the clearing to the other. He knew that Fern and her mum and dad would be coming to visit for her birthday, and was really looking forward to showing off with his bow and arrows, but he had to think of a nice present for Fern.

He wandered down to the edge of the clearing and sat down on the river-bank. He could always think better sitting there, listening to the soft whisper of the water, throwing the occasional pebble into the river and watching the ripples sparkling and spreading wider and wider across the surface.

The sparkling of the sunlight on the water stirred Chuggalug's memory. Yes! He remembered how Fern had admired the crystals, glittering in the flames of their torches at the side of the lake in the huge cavern, when they had been trapped by the earthquake. Oh yes, the earthquake. He remembered how scary it had been in the dark, before

Boing Boing came to their rescue. Maybe not…but they had eventually found their way out, so if he could find the cave entrance in the forest again…yes! He would go into the forest and look for the cave entrance. It couldn't be that hard to find, and he would collect the nicest crystal for Fern. She would love it.

Chuggalug knew that he should really tell his Mum or Dad where he was going, or wait till Boing Boing was with him, but he was so excited at the thought of the crystals that he scampered off alone into the forest to find the cave entrance. He noticed that, away towards the mountains, the sky was darkening, black clouds promising rain, but they were far off and he would be back home before it came. He searched further and further from the clearing and deeper and deeper into the forest, trying desperately to remember where it had been, but nothing looked familiar. He realised that when he had come home from the cave mouth the last time, Boing Boing had taken them home, and he hadn't really been paying attention to the way they had gone. Not that he was worried. Oh no. His head was full of the excitement of finding a beautiful, sparkly crystal for Fern. He ploughed on regardless, searching for the cave entrance.

Chuggalug was walking along a dried up river bed, and had almost given up hope, when two things happened at once. He spotted the cave entrance in front of him and heard the huge roar of a giant dinosaur behind him. Almost jumping out of his skin, he felt the hot breath of the monster as it roared again. He looked round and saw that a giant tyrannosaurus rex was right behind him, its huge mouth wide open, and its short stumpy front legs, with their powerful claws, raised ready to snatch him up.

In an instant Chuggalug took the only escape. He leapt forward and dived head first into the narrow cave opening. Tumbling down on a slope of small pebbles he came to a stop just inside the cave mouth, on his back with his feet towards the entrance hole.

Tyrannosaurus pushed his snout against the hole, trying to force his way into the cave after the boy. Chuggalug saw the rows of huge teeth and the great sharp claws of the beast as it furiously tried to bite and claw its way into the cave after him. But the hole was too small and the clawing, roaring giant was unable to get to the boy. Eventually, after what seemed like an age, Chuggalug was relieved when it gave up and lumbered away from the cave mouth, growling and snorting, into the forest.

Sitting quietly in the cave, Chuggalug listened and listened to make sure that the great beast had really gone, and wasn't just waiting for him to stick his head out and pounce.

After a while he crawled up the pebble slope and very cautiously peered over the top. It seemed all quiet. He then saw, to his horror, that in his dive into the cave, he had dropped his torch, which he needed to explore the cave. The stick, with the end wrapped in skins soaked in tar, had dropped from his waist and was lying there on the river bed, near the mouth of the cave but just too far away for him to reach.

Chuggalug carefully checked all round the trees and bushes outside the cave, watching for any movement, or sign that tyrannosaurus, or anything else, was lurking, waiting for him to come out. Satisfied that it was all clear he crawled out of the cave and, grabbing the torch, quickly returned to the safety of the dark cavern.

Lighting his torch using the sparks from two flint stones, the way he had seen his dad do many times, Chuggalug stared in wonder at the beauty of the enormous cavern. He had forgotten just how amazing it was. The flame from his torch made the water of the lake shimmer, the reflections rippling across the roof high above and the crystals embedded in the rock sparkling like stars in the night sky.

He also saw, as he stumbled down the pebble slope and along the lakeside pebble beach, that dotted among the pebbles he was walking on crystals and highly polished pebbles glistened in the torchlight, each one seemingly more beautiful than the last, making his choice of one to take for Fern more and more difficult. He picked one, only to throw it away as he spotted a nicer one just a little bit further into the cave. After a while Chuggalug came to what looked like a solid wall of rock and rubble, blocking the cave and holding back the lake water. He realised that this was the fall of rock which had trapped him and Fern during the earthquake the last time he had been down here. He reluctantly decided to make his way back.

Then he saw it. A highly polished pebble about the size of his hand was lying right at his feet. It was shining with green, brown, blue, yellow and white stone, having obviously been formed of many different types of rock. But what made it even more beautiful were the many small crystals embedded in the stone, glittering in the light. Chuggalug knew he had found the perfect present for Fern's birthday. He wrapped it up and placed it carefully in the skin bag which hung over his shoulder.

It was as he turned to head back towards the cave mouth that Chuggalug first noticed that his feet were wet. He had been so engrossed in his find that he had been unaware of the water slowly rising. He became slightly anxious as he made his way back along the lake side, holding his torch high to light his way. He became much more anxious when he saw that the water was rising faster and faster and heard the roar of what sounded like a waterfall getting louder and louder as he got nearer the cave exit.

He was horrified when he reached the cave mouth and saw that the waterfall was in fact a torrent of water roaring into the cave, filling the cave entrance and roaring down the pebble slope into the lake, which was rapidly rising, the surface getting nearer and nearer to the roof of the cavern. Chuggalug remembered the dark storm clouds, and the dried up river bed. The rain had come and the river was no longer dry but rushing headlong into the cavern, filling up the underground lake.

Taking a deep breath, Chuggalug crawled into the roaring water and started to force his way up, against the rushing torrent towards the cave entrance, holding the torch up out of the water as far as possible. The water was powerful and very cold but he slowly, slowly made his way towards the exit and safety. As he was almost at the top of the slope he realised that the lake surface had risen behind him, and that he was in fact floating on the surface of the water which had reached to within inches of the cave roof. He had just decided that he would have to swim under the water and against the strong current to have any chance of getting out.

As Chuggalug took a deep breath and prepared to throw his torch away to slip under the water, terrifyingly he found himself being sucked away from the exit and back into the cavern towards the centre of the lake. He rolled over onto his back and held the flaming torch as high as he could. He saw the roof of the cave rushing past him and getting further away as the water raced along faster and faster, the level dropping as it went.

Chuggalug knew that the storm water had filled the cavern so full that the huge body of water had burst the earthquake dam he had seen earlier, but as he rushed along, carried helplessly by the water as it raced through caves and tunnels he had no idea where it was taking him or how long it would be before he saw daylight again. He raced along, carried by the torrent. Along tunnels, with the roof only inches from his face, round bends and through great caverns, their roofs too high up to be seen in the torchlight.

Then, suddenly he was blinded as the water burst out of the cave into the bright sunshine. He was in the middle of a fast flowing river, its waters swollen by the sudden flood from the underground lake. He was carried along by the current and saw that the river he was in had joined another river, also swollen by the sudden rush of water but not so fiercely flowing. Looking at the bank for a suitable place to swim ashore,

Chuggalug realised that some of the things he was looking at were familiar. Then it dawned on him. He was in the River Nethy, and was almost at the point where it flowed past the clearing with the tree house. Home! As the clearing came into view he swam to the bank, pulled himself out and lay on the grass in the warm sunshine.

He was still lying there when he heard Fern laughing and running towards him from the tree house. "There you are," she shouted. "I've been looking for you all over. We've come to take you to our home for my birthday. Oh you're all wet! Have you been for a swim?"

"You could say that" said Chuggalug, smiling to himself as he

thought about the adventure he had just had, and felt the beautiful pebble, still safe inside his bag. It had been scary and exciting, but worth it to get such a special birthday gift.

Birthday

Chuggalug and Fern were really excited, and looking forward to the journey to the caves where Fern lived with her mum and dad. It took them through the forest, following the river, and up toward the mountains of Cairngorm, which Chuggalug often looked out at from his bedroom window in the tree house.

It was a long way, but they were going to celebrate Fern's birthday, which they knew would be fun and Chuggalug had planned a few surprises for Fern as they travelled through the great forest. He had sent his best friend Boing Boing, the huge sabre-toothed tiger on ahead to tell as many of his forest friends as he could find that they were coming, so that they could meet them and he could introduce them to Fern and their parents, none of whom had any idea of the great friends he had made during his adventures in the forest.

After what seemed like ages they were all ready to set off. Chuggalug and Fern skipped on ahead along the river side and into the forest, hardly hearing as their dads called to them to take their time and to be careful. They trekked on and on through the huge forest, listening to the screeches and squawks of small unknown creatures close by among the trees and shrubs, and, now and then, the distant roar of a much, much bigger and more dangerous monster somewhere far off in the forest.

Eventually, as they reached a large clearing in the trees, beside the river, Chuggalug's dad called to them that it was time to stop and rest. They all sat down at the riverbank to share some food which Chuggalug's mum had prepared. After they had eaten, Chuggalug and Fern ran off across the clearing to play. They had just reached the centre of the clearing when two things happened. Chuggalug's dad gave a loud warning shout and a huge shadow swept across the sunny clearing. Chuggalug and Fern looked over to his dad who was pointing up into the sky and waving to them to run towards him.

Fern looked up and screamed. An enormous pteranadon was swooping down towards them from the clear sunny sky. Fern turned to run away, but stopped in her tracks when she heard Chuggalug shout to her to wait. Chuggalug's dad was astonished when he saw that Chuggalug wasn't screaming or running towards him, but jumping up and down in the centre of the clearing, waving his arms at the great swooping creature.

Chuggalug's dad grabbed his spear as the pteranadon landed in the clearing, but they were all totally amazed at what happened then. Chuggalug was talking to the creature, which was sitting on the ground, tilting its head to one side then the other, listening to him. Fern was fixed to the spot, staring at Chuggalug and the pteranadon, listening and unable to believe what she was hearing.

"Hi, Toby," called Chuggalug. "It's great to see you again. This is my cousin Fern. We're travelling to her home near the mountains because it's her birthday. That's our mums and dads over there, and the little dinosaur is Elgin, Fern's friend."

"I know," replied Toby the pteranadon. "Boing Boing told me all about Fern's birthday, and that you would all be travelling this way. I thought that you and Fern might like to come flying with me."

Chuggalug's and Fern's parents had walked over, and laughed when they heard Chuggalug and Toby talking. Their mums were a bit concerned when they heard what Toby was suggesting, but after Toby assured them that he would look after the two youngsters, they agreed, much to Chuggalug and Fern's delight.

With much giggling and excitement Chuggalug and Fern climbed on to Toby's back, Chuggalug hanging on to the great beast's long neck and Fern with her arms round Chuggalug's waist.

Toby turned round slowly and carefully, to face into the warm wind, spread his huge wings and, with a mighty leap, took off into the breeze and soared up and up into the sunny blue sky. Fern squealed with delight as

she saw the clearing with their parents and little Elgin get smaller and smaller as they rose higher and higher. She held on tight as Toby dived down and swooped low and fast over the group and then climbed higher and higher till they were just tiny figures far below.

Chuggalug and Fern looked all round. They could see for miles and miles in every direction, from the dark mountains of Cairngorm to the mighty River Spey and on and on to the great loch far away.

"Where do you two want to go?" called Toby, as he circled high above the forest. "I don't mind. Anywhere!" squealed Fern. "I had no idea you had such great friends,

Chuggalug. This is the best birthday ever." "I know," called Chuggalug. "Let's go to the great loch. There's another surprise for you there."

Toby turned towards the loch, far away to the north, gliding effortlessly over the lush green carpet of the forest, far below. Chuggalug and Fern shouted and pointed as they spotted huge dinosaurs among the trees and a large waterfall in the river as it flowed northwards towards the sea.

They soon felt Toby gliding gently down and down and saw that they were above the waters of the great loch which seemed to stretch on and on as far as the eye could see. Chuggalug called to Toby and pointed down to a stretch of pebbly beach. Toby turned slowly and very gently came in to land on the beach, next to the sparkling loch.

Chuggalug and Fern scrambled down from Toby's back and stood on the beach, scanning the shimmering water and listening to the silence. "This is beautiful," whispered Fern, looking all round. "What a lovely surprise." But Chuggalug had scampered down the beach, and was rolling a large tree trunk into the water. "Come on," he shouted. "You haven't seen the surprise yet."

Chuggalug sat on the tree trunk, his feet dangling into the water on each side. "Come on! Get on!" he laughed. Fern climbed on to the log and Chuggalug paddled with his feet away from the beach and out into the loch.

Fern sat on the log, her feet dangling in the cool water. The only sound was the lapping of the water on the log. It was really beautiful, the shimmering, sparkling water and the majestic mountains all around, but she couldn't help feeling slightly scared. Where was Chuggalug taking them? She knew the loch must be very deep, and it was much too wide to paddle right across. Whatever could the next surprise be, way out here in the middle of the great loch?

A disturbance on the smooth surface of the water, near the log made Fern look round quickly. She nearly capsized the log as she grabbed hold of Chuggalug. "What was that?" she whispered urgently. "Don't worry," smiled Chuggalug. "Just watch."

Fern clutched Chuggalug's shirt even tighter as a huge head appeared slowly out of the water. It rose and rose, higher and higher on its long neck and looked down quietly at Chuggalug and Fern on the log. Then, to Fern's amazement Chuggalug laughed. "Hi, Nessie!" he called cheerfully. Fern's mouth opened even wider when the huge monster replied. "Hi, Chuggalug!" The voice was deep and sounded just like Fern thought a sea monster should. It was also much friendlier than she expected. She found that she was not frightened at all now.

"This is my cousin Fern," said Chuggalug. "Fern, this is my friend Nessie; he's a plesiosaur. It's Fern's birthday soon, Nessie."

"Is it really?" said Nessie. "So what about a swim round the loch for a birthday treat?" Fern looked away up the loch. "I'm afraid I couldn't swim that far," she said quietly. Nessie lowered his huge head next to hers. "Don't worry, Fern. I'll do the swimming. You two just get on my back and hold on tight."

The plesiosaur slowly and carefully swam over beside the log. His huge body rose in the water so Chuggalug and Fern could climb off the log and sit astride his back. Fern saw that Nessie had two huge flippers on each side of his enormous body and once they were both safely settled on his back, first the front flippers, then the back ones drove them powerfully through the water, and off up the loch, leaving a long V-shaped wake behind them.

Fern laughed and squealed with delight as they forged up the loch in the warm sunshine, her hair blowing out behind her in the slight breeze. She threw her head back, marvelling at the massive mountains soaring high above them on each side of the loch, mesmerised as they slowly and silently drifted behind them as they went.

She squealed even louder when,

at one point, another two heads and necks, even bigger than Nessie's rose out of the water and swam along beside them. "That's Nessie's mum and dad!" called Chuggalug, waving to the two giant plesiosaurs.

Eventually, Nessie turned round in a great wide turn, and headed for the side of the loch. Chuggalug pointed up to the sky, and Fern, looking up, saw that Toby had been flying overhead and was swooping down to land on a large rock beside the beach. Nessie took them right in next to the beach and they scrambled down into the shallow water. "Thank you! Thank you!" laughed Fern excitedly to Nessie, as she reached the pebbly beach and turned to wave goodbye. "This is turning out to be the best birthday ever!" "Bye, Fern. Bye, Chuggalug," called Nessie, his long neck slowly disappearing into the water as he backed away from the side of the loch into the deep water. "Come again soon and we'll go for another swim." The huge head disappeared, leaving only a few round ripples on the glassy surface. Chuggalug and Fern stood quietly watching the ripples for a few moments, then turned and walked up the beach to where Toby was waiting.

"Right. Let's get you two back to your mums and dads," said Toby as they clambered excitedly on to his back. "Hold on!" he shouted, spreading his huge wings and launching himself forward into the air. He swooped low over the loch and Chuggalug and Fern waved goodbye to Nessie, whose head was just disappearing under the water. With a few flaps of his powerful wings he then soared up, away from the loch and over the mountains, back towards the forest where they knew their parents would be waiting.

Once again Fern and Chuggalug were amazed at the sight of the forest below, stretching in every direction as far as they could see. They heard the roars of giant dinosaurs far below them, and were a little bit scared when Toby swooped down low over the head of an enormous and very fierce looking tyrannosaurus rex, which stretched up on its back legs and roared up at them as they flew overhead.

Soon Chuggalug realised they were flying above familiar forest. He pointed down at the river below, which he knew was the River Nethy, flowing from the mountains of Cairngorm, past the cave where Fern lived and on down past the clearing with the great oak tree where he lived, on its way to the mighty River Spey. Toby flew on towards the mountains, until, far below, Chuggalug and Fern spotted the clearing beside the cave mouth where Fern lived, and their parents standing waving up at them. They both yelled and waved back as Toby gently circled lower and lower. As they neared the ground they saw little Elgin scampering round and round, obviously happy and excited to see Fern again.

Toby landed softly on the grass and the two youngsters scrambled down and ran frantically to their parents, each trying to tell the story of their wonderful adventure, the words tumbling out in an excited stream until Chuggalug's dad held up his hands, laughing, "Wait a minute you two. Calm down! We'll hear all about it later, don't you think you both have something to say to Toby?"

Chuggalug and Fern stopped in mid sentence and both turned round, running to Toby, throwing their arms round his long neck. "Thank you!" said Chuggalug. "Thank you very much Toby!" said Fern. "You've made this the best birthday ever." "You're welcome," called Toby, turning into the wind and spreading his enormous leathery wings. "I've enjoyed it too. We must do it again soon." "Yes please!" called Chuggalug and Fern together. They watched as Toby leapt into the air and rose higher and higher into the clear blue sky, soon becoming a dot in the far distance.

Fern turned and ran towards Elgin, hugging the little dinosaur, who snuggled into her, obviously delighted to have his best friend back with him.

Chuggalug looked round the

clearing, suddenly realising that his best friend Boing Boing wasn't about. He turned to his dad. "Have you seen Boing Boing?" he asked. "Where can he be?" His dad smiled down at him. "Don't worry," he said, smiling. "He'll be here soon. He went off to try to find more of your forest friends. I'm beginning to wonder just how many friends you have in the forest."

A loud roar from the forest made them turn round. "It's Boing Boing!" shouted Chuggalug. "I knew he'd come!" More roaring, and some very loud rumbling and crashing told them that Boing Boing was not alone. Chuggalug and Fern jumped up and down and squealed with delight as they saw Boing Boing, accompanied by his four cubs Tim, Tam, Tom and Tum, all now grown into huge sabre-toothed tigers, and their mum. The youngsters' mums and dads watched in amazement as the six fierce looking tigers surrounded Chuggalug and Fern, nudging them and licking their faces, making them giggle.

The reason for the loud crashing and rumbling then became apparent. First one, then two, then three and then a whole crowd of enormous heads and great long necks appeared from the forest. Chuggalug could hardly believe his eyes. "Derandan!" he squealed. "Fern! Come and meet my friends Derandan the diplodocus and his herd. They once saved me from the velociraptors." Fern giggled as the huge heads came down and all seemed to try to nuzzle her at the same time.

Suddenly Chuggalug remembered. "Fern! Come here. I've got another surprise for you. I really hope you like it." He reached into the pouch on his belt and pulled out the glittering, many coloured pebble he'd found in the cavern. He handed it to Fern who looked at it in her palm. "It's beautiful," she whispered. "Thank you, Chuggalug." She looked round the clearing at her mum and dad, Chuggalug and his mum and dad, little Elgin, Boing Boing and the rest of the sabre-toothed tigers, the herd of diplodocus, and remembering the adventure with Toby and Nessie, she thought she must be the luckiest girl in the world.

The Move

Chuggalug and his parents were still staying with Fern and her mum and dad in their great cave near the mountains. They had been there for a few days, since Fern's birthday, and were planning their journey home. But Chuggalug had a feeling that his dad and Fern's dad were worried about something. He had seen them, one day looking up at the high mountains and when he looked, he saw a dark plume of thick smoke rising from the mountains away in the distance. "It's only a fire," he thought to himself, "And it's so far away; it can't harm us down here." He shrugged and put it to the back of his mind, thinking instead of the exciting journey ahead.

While they were packing all their belongings for the journey, Chuggalug sat at the edge of the clearing, watching the smoke plume far away. It seemed to be getting thicker and was rising high into the sky. "It must be a really big fire," he thought. "I hope all my forest friends are safe." He was about to turn and walk back to the cave when something very strange happened. So strange that he thought he'd imagined it. A low rumble seemed to come from under his feet, and he was sure he felt the ground move. At the same time he saw a large ripple disturb the smooth glassy surface of the river, breaking gently on the bank next to him. He turned and quickly walked off, to tell his dad what had just happened.

He had only reached the middle of the clearing when Toby the pteranadon suddenly appeared above him and landed in the clearing. "Hi, Toby!" called Chuggalug, pleased to see his friend again. "I'll go and get Fern. She'll be so happy to see you."

But Toby seemed anxious. "I need to speak to your dad," he said quietly. "Can you go and get him?"

Chuggalug ran off into the cave. He found his dad still packing up for the journey home. "Dad," said Chuggalug as quietly as he could. "Can you come outside?"

"In a while," replied his dad.

"I'm still busy packing."

"But dad. It's Toby. He's outside. He seems worried about something and he wants to speak to you."

"Okay," said his dad. "Let's go." Chuggalug walked out with his dad to where Toby was waiting.

"Hello, Toby. What's worrying you?" said Chuggalug's dad. Toby looked up at the mountain and the growing smoke plume. "It's that," he said. "It's not a fire, it's a volcano, and it's about to erupt. It's getting worse every day. All the animals are leaving the mountain. You must all leave here and get as far away as possible before the whole mountain explodes. And it could happen any time." As if to emphasise Toby's warning, with another deep rumble, the whole clearing seemed to shake and lots of pebbles showered down from the cliff above the cave mouth, clattering into the clearing all around them.

"Right! Thanks, Toby" said Chuggalug's dad. "You get off now out of danger. We'll get out of here and head down the river as fast as we can. Come on Chuggalug. We've no time to lose if we're to get away safely." Chuggalug followed him as he headed back into the cave to warn the others.

They decided they would all travel downstream together in Ferns dad's boat, with as much stuff as they could safely pack in, and that Fern, Chuggalug and Elgin would travel in the smaller boat Fern's dad had built for her. The two boats would be tied together for safety. They would travel down river, into the River Spey and on and on as far as they needed to, till it was safe to stop and set up camp. Little did they know how terrible the eruption was going to be, or how far they were going to travel!

They were still busily loading the boat when the first eruption came. Looking up at the mountains, they saw that the huge plume of smoke was now much higher. It had a bright orange glow, and they saw flashes of lightning playing all round it. A few seconds later the deafening roar of the explosion hit them and the ground began to shake. Chuggalug's dad shouted for everyone to run inside the cave, as a shower of small stones and then larger boulders started to clatter and crash down from the cliff face.

When the ground stopped shaking and things seemed a bit quieter, they all ran to the river and climbed into the boats. As they pushed off into the river, Fern looked back and wondered if she would ever see her cave again and Chuggalug wondered if he would ever see his tree house again. They didn't get long to daydream as the deafening roar of another explosion from the mountain told them that the eruption was getting worse.

Chuggalug and Fern clung on to

the sides of the small boat as it was carried downstream. All around them the forest was alight, as lumps of red hot rock, thrown out by the volcano set fire to the grass and trees. They watched, horrified as the water hissed and boiled, sending up plumes of steam as some of the rocks splashed into the river.

But even worse were the fires. It seemed that the whole forest was ablaze, as the red hot rocks rained down among the trees and shrubs, setting them alight. The strong warm wind fanned the flames this way and that, spreading the fire from tree to tree with frightening speed. They could hear the roars and screeches of large dinosaurs and small forest

creatures, as they also desperately tried to escape the nightmare all around them.

They sailed on and on, swept along by the river current, out of the River Nethy and out into the mighty River Spey, which somehow felt safer. It was much wider and, although the forest fire still raged all around them, the scorching heat seemed to be more bearable in the middle of the great river. Chuggalug lay in the bottom of the boat, watching Fern hugging little Elgin, and wondered and hoped that Boing Boing and all the rest of his forest friends were safe.

The two boats drifted on and on downstream. The great river became wider and wider. After what seemed like ages, the current appeared to be outrunning the terrible forest fires. The air felt cooler and fresher. Chuggalug sat up and looked around. As he looked back it was a terrible sight. The forest was ablaze as far as the eye could see, huge flames leaping into the sky, high above the trees. The whole sky behind them was a thick black pall of smoke and away in the distance the orange glow was brighter then darker as the volcano erupted again and again.

But when Chuggalug looked forward everything was so different. The sun shone brightly out of a blue cloudless sky. The green river banks sloped up into the lush shrubbery and trees of the forest. Chuggalug felt the

excitement inside him grow as he realised that, wherever the river was taking them, it was to a new home and a new life.

Soon Elgin sat up and, looking out at the river bank, became excited too. "I know where we are!" he squealed. "We're nearly there!"

"Where?" asked Chuggalug and Fern together.

"We're nearly at my old home, where I lived before I met you!" He rushed back and forth in the small boat, which started to rock in the water.

"Sit down, Elgin!" laughed Fern. "You'll capsize the boat, and you know you hate the water."

"Okay," said Elgin, sitting back

down. "But we'll need to warn your dads to get to the bank of the river before we reach the sea, or we'll be carried out, away from the land."

Chuggalug stood up in the front of the boat and shouted the warning to his dad, who waved back to show he understood. Very soon they saw their dads paddling their boat towards the bank, pulling the smaller boat behind them. They reached the riverbank just before the river widened and flowed out into the sea. They all climbed out of the boats and quietly walked together to the brow of the sand dunes. They looked out to sea and marvelled at the water stretching right to the horizon. They looked along the beach, fringed by the forest shrubs and trees. They all knew that they would have to find a safe place to build their new homes and that a new life stretched before them.

And when Chuggalug heard the loud roar of a huge sabre-toothed tiger approaching from the forest, he knew that his new life was going to be okay.